Tornado Brain

Also by Cat Patrick

Just Like Fate, with Suzanne Young

The Originals

Revived

Forgotten

TORNADO BRAIN

CAT PATRICK

putnam

G. P. Putnam's Sons

G. P. Putnam's Sons

An imprint of Penguin Random House LLC, New York

Visit us online at penguinrandomhouse.com

Library of Congress Cataloging-in-Publication Data
Names: Patrick, Cat, author.
Title: Tornado brain / Cat Patrick.
Description: New York: G. P. Putnam's Sons, [2020] | Summary: "A neurodivergent 7th grader is determined to find her missing best friend before it's too late"—Provided by publisher.
Identifiers: LCCN 2019048583 (print) | LCCN 2019048584 (ebook) |
ISBN 9781984815316 (hardcover) | ISBN 9781984815323 (ebook)
Subjects: CYAC: Missing children—Fiction. | Best friends—Fiction. | Friendship—Fiction. | Asperger's syndrome—Fiction. | Attention-deficit hyperactivity disorder—Fiction. | Sensory disorders—Fiction. | Family life—Washington (State)—Fiction. | Washington (State)—Fiction.
Classification: LCC PZ7.P2746 Tor 2020 (print) | LCC PZ7.P2746 (ebook) | DDC [Fic]—dc23
LC record available at https://lccn.loc.gov/2019048583
LC ebook record available at https://lccn.loc.gov/2019048584

Printed in the United States of America
ISBN 9781984815316

10 9 8 7 6 5 4 3 2 1

Design by Eileen Savage | Text set in Alda OT

For the remarkable Adiline M.

What a force of nature you are.

Tornado Brain

prologue

Myth: Tornadoes only move northeast.

PEOPLE USED TO believe that tornadoes only move in one direction—to the northeast—but that's not true. Sometimes they go southwest. Sometimes they touch down and don't go anywhere, getting sucked right back up into the sky. That's disappointing. Sometimes they zig and sometimes they zag. Tornadoes are unpredictable.

If a tornado was in middle school, it might get a lot of weird looks from other kids. Its counselor might call its behavior "unexpected." Its mom might try to get it to move in the same direction as the other tornadoes just to fit in. But maybe the tornado doesn't care about fitting in—even if it means not having a lot of friends.

I can relate because I used to have one friend but now I don't. It's complicated.

I met her during a tornado.

It was the first week of kindergarten. My memories from back then are foggy because I was just a little kid and also my memory is weird, but here's how I think it went. Everyone was at recess and I was circling the outside of the play area alone, thinking of roller coasters because I was obsessed with them then, feeling my way along the chain link because I liked the way my fingers dropped into the spaces between the links and the way my hand smelled like metal afterward. Not a lot of people like that smell.

Sometimes I don't notice things at all and sometimes I notice things too much. That day, I noticed when the wind turbine at the far end of the playground stopped turning. I live in Long Beach, Washington, and it's known for being windy—so windy that there's an international kite festival every August—so when the turbine stopped, it was different. I notice things that are different. The creepy green-gray circular clouds behind the unmoving turbine were different, too. That's called a mesocyclone, which is a word I like.

I don't know if any other kid on the playground saw the twister fall from the funnel cloud that day. I was probably the only one who was looking up instead of playing tetherball or hanging upside down from the monkey bars or something. Being upside down makes my head feel funny.

I watched as the tornado hit the ground and started bumping toward us, tossing things that looked like bugs but were really recycling bins. The emergency system was loud, so I covered my ears. Kids ran inside but I didn't run; I walked . . . in the direction of the tornado. I took my hands off my ears and heard the train sound, far away at first, then louder and louder. The tiny bottom of the tornado got bigger as it collected stuff, pulling up and tossing small trees and even sucking up a utility pole, sending sparks into the sky like fireworks.

I was sucked up, too—by an adult. He grabbed me and started running toward the school. I watched the tornado rip out the far part of the playground fence, which is probably the coolest thing I've ever seen in my life.

"What is wrong with you?" the adult shouted, too close to my ear.

An audiologist once told me that I have better-than-average hearing, so it hurt. If you don't know what an audiologist is, it's a doctor who studies hearing loss and balance issues related to the ears. I don't have either of those things, but still I went to one—along with many other doctors that have *ologist* at the end of their titles.

I cupped my hands over my ears, but I could still hear him shouting: "You need to listen to directions! You could have been killed!"

"It's not my fault," I said. "No one told me any directions."

I bounced along in the teacher's arms, watching the turbine pick up speed until I couldn't see it anymore because it had a tornado wrapped around it like a big tornado hug. The teacher banged through the doors and we were inside the school, running down the hall toward the cafeteria. Without the distraction of the tornado, I noticed his painful grip around my thighs and back. I stiffened and started to slip from his grasp. By the time we made it to the cafeteria, where all the other kids and teachers were hiding under tables, he was holding me only under the arms, my board-straight legs swinging like a pendulum in my flowered capris. My armpits hurt when he finally set me down next to a table in the middle of the room.

"Found her," he said to my teacher. I don't remember her name. I didn't like her very much.

"Come under, Frances," she said. "Sit next to me. It's going to be okay."

"My name is Frankie," I said, crawling under the table. "And I know."

"You gave us a scare, Frankie," she said, stroking my hair. I honestly don't know why people think that's comforting.

"Don't touch me," I snapped, scooting as far away from her as I could get. She looked surprised at first, then frowned and turned to talk to the man who'd carried me.

"I was just watching," I said softly to myself.

"Watching what?" a girl on my right asked. She had braided orange hair with red bows tied at the ends, too

4

many freckles all over her cheeks and forehead, and a terri-fied expression.

"I saw the tornado!" I said.

"I want my mommy," she said before putting her thumb in her mouth. Now she looked like a baby. "Is it going to get us?" she asked around her thumb, making it harder to under-stand her. "Will we die? I don't want to die, I want to be a singer. Do you want to hold hands?"

I definitely did not want to touch the hand that she had in her mouth, and I was overwhelmed by her questions.

"What?" I asked, blinking.

"My name is Colette," she answered.

"That's not what I asked."

"What's your name?"

"Frankie."

"I'm scared," she said.

I wasn't feeling scared until the train sound got loud enough to rattle the windows. Then Colette hugged me, and I let her without thinking. Predictably unpredictable, the tornado would turn southwest at the last minute and just miss our school before being whooshed back into the clouds, but of course we didn't know that at the time. I found out later that it was an EF3 on the Enhanced Fujita Scale, which is classified as "intense." I didn't know that then either.

Then I just knew that I was scared, too. I squashed my cheek against Colette's, my arms around her. She was probably the first person other than my family members I'd ever hugged.

"If we don't die, let's be friends," Colette said.

"Okay," I said.

We didn't die, so we were friends.

PART I

Fri-yay

chapter 1

Fact: In some parts of the country,
middle schools have built-in tornado shelters.

COLETTE WENT MISSING on the second Friday in April,
almost at the end of seventh grade. It was seven and a half
years after the tornado in kindergarten, and Colette and I
hadn't been friends anymore for two months.

Before any of us knew she was missing, it was a normal
morning. My mom appeared in my doorway at six thirty.
Opening my eyes and seeing a person in the doorway made
my heart jump.

"I hate it when you do that!" I complained.

"Good morning, Frankie," Mom said in a soothing voice.
"Time to get ready for school."

I closed my eyes again.

I'd had trouble falling asleep the night before because
I'd been playing something over in my head and when I'm

thinking too much at bedtime, my brain doesn't turn off and go to sleep. Plus, I'd forgotten to take the vitamin that helps me sleep. And then I'd woken up twice during the night for no reason, once at two thirty and once at five. It's hard for me to get back to sleep when that happens. Adding it all together, I'd probably had about four hours of sleep.

I rubbed my eyes with my fists, then scooted deeper under the covers, wishing my mom would go away. But I could still smell the scents she'd brought in with her: nice shampoo and disgusting coffee. I pictured a cartoon drawing of coffee-smell pouncing on a cartoon drawing of nice-shampoo-smell. The nice-shampoo-smell fought back and shoved the coffee-smell off, then . . .

"Are you awake, Frankie?" my mom said.

I am now.

Lately, I'd been concentrating on using manners, so I focused on not yelling that I wanted her to leave so I could wake up in peace. *Do not yell,* I told myself, my voice loud in my head. *Do not tell her to get out. Make your voice match hers.*

I opened my eyes and looked at her sideways because I was on my side.

"Hi," I groaned, my tired, grumpy, scratchy voice not sounding like hers at all. She ignored it.

"It's Friday!" Mom said. "Or, since it's your early-release day, should I say, Fri-*yay*?"

We got out of school at 11:25 a.m. on Fridays, so we were

only there for three hours and five minutes, or three class periods—and one of them was homeroom—unless you were an overachiever who'd chosen to take zero period. Zero period is the optional period *before* homeroom and it's way too early for me.

"Uh-huh," I growled, rolling away and pulling the covers over my shoulder. "I'm awake, you can leave now."

"You know the rule," Mom said. "I can't leave until you're upright."

That is the stupidest rule ever! I shouted in my head. It was almost painful not to say it out loud, but I thought about manners and counted to ten and managed not to yell. I threw off my covers and got out of bed, hunched forward, my fists clenched, frowning. But upright.

"There," I said.

"Thank you," my mom said, which bugged me.

I guess I should say right now that I love my mom, so you don't get the wrong idea. She's not mean or anything. I just . . . Things bother me really easily. Or they don't bother me at all. I tend to have extreme feelings one way or the other, not usually in the middle. Maybe that's why I'm sometimes unhappy. I don't know. Anyway.

When my mom finally left, I put on my softest skinny jeans, the ones that I wore at least twice a week. Today, I noticed the seams digging against the sides of my thighs and I hated it, so I changed into a different pair. I pulled on my black hoodie with the thumbholes, testing out the feeling of that for a second, deciding it was okay. The seams of the new pants bugged me, too, so I changed into leggings. They had a hole in the knee but felt okay. I stuck my long fingernail in the hole and made it bigger.

I shoved my unfinished homework into my backpack, then went to brush my teeth. In the mirror, a girl with messy, chin-length hair and too-long bangs, bloodshot brown eyes with dark circles under them, and cracked lips stared back at me. I looked down at my toothbrush: there was a hair on it. I threw it away and leaned over to get a new one out of the cabinet. While I was searching, I found a headband I used to wear all the time when I was younger. I'd never wear it now, but I tried it on, wishing I could text a picture of myself to Colette because I looked hilarious, but I couldn't because we weren't friends anymore. I left the bathroom, dropping the headband on the floor.

I pulled my hood up over my bedhead. From the mini-fridge in my room, I got out the milk, then made myself a bowl of the single brand of cereal I like in the world. I checked my TwisterLvr feed and read about an EF2-category tornado that'd happened in Birmingham, Alabama, the night before. I didn't check my other social media anymore because I didn't want to see all the pictures of Colette and her other friends.

I got my jacket and left. I wanted to ride my favorite

yellow beach cruiser to school, but it wasn't where it was supposed to be, so I had to walk. Only a minute or two into the walk, my phone buzzed in my pocket.

Do you have your backpack?

I turned around to get it. At the door, Mom held out the pack in one hand and a protein bar in the other. Her dark hair was in a tight bun that looked uncomfortable. I patted the top of my head.

"Don't forget to eat it, please."

"I won't," I said, turning to leave again. She was always reminding me to eat. She didn't remind other people to eat—just me. I guess maybe I needed to be reminded sometimes, but it was still annoying.

"I don't want you to get hangry," she said.

Did you know that the word *hangry* is officially in the dictionary now? It is. I looked it up.

"I'm old enough to know when I need to eat," I complained.

"Yes, at thirteen, you *are* old enough," she said in a way that made me think she was trying to make a point. "Did you brush your teeth?"

"Yes," I said, not totally sure whether I had or not. "Bye."

"Have a great day, Frankie! I love you!"

I made a sound and left again, taking the beach path so I could shout into the wind if I felt like it. I didn't this morning, but I like having options. I like choosing what I get to do because it feels like people are always bossing me around. The only thing is, the beach path takes longer than just walking straight to school. It's like turning the route into an obtuse triangle instead of a line from point A to point B.

Do you know what that is? It's geometry, which I like.

I was late to school so often that the hall monitor didn't blink. I left some books and the uneaten protein bar in my locker, which I don't share with anyone because I don't like when their books touch mine, and left a trail of sand like bread crumbs as I walked down the carpeted hallway to homeroom. The bell rang when I was about halfway to class, and Ms. Garrett didn't say anything when I walked in.

All the other kids were already at their desks, most of them socializing. That's a thing I'm not good at, probably because I don't like *chitchat*—the word itself or the act of doing it.

I sat down at my own private desk island by the window and checked my TwisterLvr account again. Nothing new had happened since the last time I'd checked, which was disappointing.

"Phones away or they're mine," Ms. Garrett said. Some people groaned, but everyone made their phones disappear. Not literally: I don't go to Hogwarts.

Ms. Garrett kept talking: "Let's all work on something productive. That means you too, Anna and Daphne. Marcus! Settle down now."

The room got quiet. Everyone took out homework, because first period is homeroom and that's what you do. I opened *Call of the Wild*, which is about a dog named Buck who lives in the freezing Yukon. Sometimes I specifically don't like books that other people tell me to read, but I liked that one even though reading it wasn't my idea.

This lady—this specialist who was always checking in with me at school—popped her head into the room. Her name is Ms. Faust and she's fine, I guess, except no one else has weird ladies checking up on them, so I pretended not to notice her and eventually she left. Ms. Faust was assigned to me or whatever, so it was her job to check in, but I didn't care. I didn't want her anywhere near me.

I was several chapters into my book when Ms. Garrett put her bony hand on my shoulder, startling me. I cringed and pulled away from her, biting my tongue so I wouldn't say anything she'd think was rude. I didn't want her to call my mom. I touched my opposite shoulder to even myself out, looking down at my notebook and noticing that I'd drawn a few tiny tornadoes while I'd been reading.

"Sorry, Frances," she said, looking embarrassed.

"My name is Frankie," I snapped accidentally. Thankfully, she let it go.

"Again, I apologize. I know you don't like when people touch you, but you didn't answer when I said your name." I strained my neck looking up at her because Ms. Garrett is skyscraper tall (not literally, of course). She kept talking. "Uh, I notice that you're reading your book for English, which is great, but I wanted to make sure you've finished your math homework. We only have a few minutes left in the period and Mr. Hubble asked me to check with you. He said that yesterday, you—"

"It's in my backpack," I interrupted, which wasn't a lie. It *was* in my backpack. It was also unfinished.

"I see," Ms. Garrett said. She tilted her head to the side like my dog does sometimes.

Behind Ms. Garrett, across the room in the regular rows, several kids were watching us. Tess smiled at me with her mouth but not her eyes, a halfway smile, which was confusing; Kai smiled at me with his mouth *and* his eyes, an all-the-way smile, which was confusing in a different way; and Mia didn't smile, just stared, which wasn't confusing in the least. I frowned at all of them and they went back to their classwork.

Ms. Garrett opened her mouth to say something else— maybe to ask to see my homework—but the announcement bell chimed, and the office lady started talking. That was unexpected, because it wasn't announcement day, which is Tuesday. And if we *had* had announcements, they would have been at the beginning of the period, not the end.

"Attention, students and staff," the office lady said. "Please proceed immediately in an orderly fashion to the auditorium for an address from Principal Golden. Thank you."

Ms. Garrett looked at me blankly for a few seconds like she was stunned, but then she told everyone to get up and move toward the auditorium. Kai smiled at me all-the-way again as he left the classroom with his friends. Confused by how I felt about that, I waited until everyone else left, too, and then went into the hall.

I watched Kai walk like he was going to wobble over, laughing so hard his eyes got watery as his friend Dillon told a story about some try-hard tourist who had wiped out at the skate park. Kai had on dark blue skate pants with cargo pockets and checkerboard slip-on sneakers and his shiny black hair looked especially interesting, like he'd been blasted by a huge gust of wind from behind and his hair had gotten stuck. I could see a scab on the back of his arm above his left elbow, which grossed me out.

Their conversation got quieter, then Dillon turned around and looked at me, so I stopped watching Kai and stared at the wall instead.

You should know that most people think Ocean View Middle School looks incredibly strange. About five years ago, when the old school was getting run-down, instead of wrecking it and building something new, they just added on. The front part with the offices, cafeteria, and math and English halls is clean and bright, but the back part with the auditorium and shop and music rooms is dark and smells like old sneakers.

I like to run my hands along walls when I walk because I don't like being surrounded by the other kids since they sometimes accidentally bump me. That's what I was doing when Tess appeared next to me.

Tall and skinny, not as tall as Ms. Garrett, though, she walked sort of bent in on herself like she was trying to be shorter. Her smooth, dark hair was parted on the side, so she had to tuck the hair-curtain behind her right ear to make eye contact. Eye contact made me uncomfortable.

"Did you get in trouble?" she asked quietly, raising her perfectly neat eyebrows. I stared at them: Eyebrows are really weird, actually. They never exactly match. There's always . . .

"Frankie?"

"Huh?"

"I asked if you got in trouble?" Tess repeated.

"For what?"

"For not doing your homework?" She practically whispered it. Tess talked super-quietly, like she didn't want anyone to hear her. I barely could.

"I did my homework," I said, which wasn't a lie. I'd done

some of my homework. And it wasn't really her business in the first place. But I managed not to tell her that. Despite getting hungrier by the second, I was doing okay at manners so far today. I mean, except when I'd snapped at my teacher. But since she hadn't gotten mad, it didn't count.

"Oh, okay," Tess said. "Sorry."

Mia nudged Tess and told her to look at something on her social feed and Tess did and they both giggled—Mia loudly and Tess softly—and I was happy not to be asked any more questions about my homework.

In the auditorium, I followed Tess and Mia down the aisle. Tess was half a head taller than Mia and Mia's butt was half a cheek bigger than Tess's. Tess walked like a normal teenager in her skinny jeans and gray T-shirt with an open sweater that looked like a blanket over it. Mia swayed her hips back and forth in her flowy jumpsuit, making her long, curly blond hair sway, too. They picked a row and I sat behind them on the end by the aisle. I looked around, not seeing where Kai was sitting.

I did notice Ms. Faust smiling at me encouragingly from where she was leaning against the far wall. I wished she'd look at someone else.

"Move over," a mean kid named Alex said, staring down at me. He was always yelling at people—a few times even teachers. I may have big emotions, but not like Alex. "Make room for other people."

"I was here first," I said, my need to sit on the aisle outweighing my desire not to get yelled at by Alex. I really don't like being surrounded. "Here," I said, moving my knees to the left so he could squeeze through.

"Whatever," Alex said, shaking his head and stepping on my foot as he shoved past me.

"Ouch!" I said loudly. He rolled his eyes and didn't apologize. I folded my arms over my chest and slumped down in my chair.

It took a while for all 323 students to sit down. Well, 322 today, but we didn't know that yet. The room felt like being on a beach when an electrical storm is coming, like you could get zapped any minute. That's figurative language—similes and metaphors and stuff. I'm trying to use it more instead of being so literal all the time because people laugh at you when you're literal.

Onstage, Principal Golden held up a hand with her middle and ring finger touching her thumb, the pointer and pinkie sticking straight up: the Quiet Coyote.

"So lame," I heard Alex say loudly. Principal Golden looked right at him in a way I wouldn't want to be looked at by the principal, and he didn't say anything else.

Principal Golden sniffed loudly into the microphone.

"Something has happened," she said, her *p*'s making irritating popping sounds in the mic. "This morning, there has been an incident. We're not sure of the details, but one of our Ocean View students is missing."

I heard the buzzing of the microphone for a couple of seconds before the entire auditorium broke out in whispers.

"Did she say missing?"

"I wonder who it is?"

"What do you think happened?"

My mind started ping-ponging from the idea of a missing student to the missing-kid posters on the bulletin board at I Scream for Ice Cream, where my biological father made me and my sister go when he visited last year even though it was the middle of winter and pouring rain and my sister is lactose intolerant. I shook my head to tune back in to what Principal Golden was saying.

" . . . investigating and we don't know anything more at this time. The police are searching the school and want to speak to select students. Rather than further disrupting this already short school day, the administration has decided to cancel class for the rest of the day. If you ride the bus, please see Mrs. Taylor in the office for instructions on . . ."

Everyone got up at once and started talking except me: I stayed in my seat, waiting for the auditorium to thin out. My row had to exit from the other side because I was blocking my end: even mean Alex went the other way, and I was glad because I didn't want my foot trampled again.

It was 9:40 and I was supposed to be starting second period, English, but instead I was going to go home. My stomach rolled with the weird feeling of change. Change is my enemy.

"She's not answering her phone."

I looked over to see Tess and Mia huddled together in the aisle, whispering to each other. "When's the last time you talked to her?"

"Last night before dinner," Mia said, spinning the ring on her middle finger. "She wasn't in zero period. I thought she slept in."

"That's not like her, though," Tess said, chewing her lip. "Her bag's not in our locker." I leaned forward so I could hear Tess better, wondering if it bugged her that Mia's curls were touching her hand. I brushed my own hand like they'd been touching mine. "Is she home sick?"

They looked at each other, both with big eyes that reminded me of a certain comic book cat, Mia's blue like a sunny day and Tess's green-gray like a cloudy one. Maybe they felt me watching them because they both looked at me at the same time.

"Have you talked to Colette?" Tess asked in her tentative voice.

"Of course I've talked to Colette," I said.

"I mean *recently*," Tess clarified. "Like, did you talk to

Colette yesterday?" Now she was pulling on the lip she'd been biting. It was distracting: I wished she'd leave her lip alone.

"No," I said, just to say something. *No* is an easy response for me.

"This is serious," Mia said, leaning forward like my therapist did sometimes. She lowered her voice. "What if it's her?"

"What if what's her?" I asked.

Mia sighed loudly. "Why are you always so spacey?"

Tess gave her a look, then explained, "Frankie, what we're asking is: What if the missing student is *Colette*?"

I stared at her without saying anything because that idea really didn't make sense to me—since I obviously didn't know at the time that the missing student *was* Colette and since I'd been mostly thinking that it felt strange being told to go home when I'd just gotten to school. This was not my normal routine.

"Come on," Mia said, pulling on Tess's arm, "let's go see if the teachers need help."

chapter 2

Myth: Twin tornadoes are extremely rare.

THE PSYCHIATRIST IS the one who labels you.

My mom picked up clothes and books and papers from the floor while I lounged on my bed, trying to ignore her, instead of being at school. I concentrated on not being annoyed about her touching my stuff because if I exploded, she'd probably make me go to the psychiatrist again.

Our deal was that if I could keep my anger and other stuff under control, I could stay off medication. And I really wanted to stay off medication: it made me sleepy or starving or spacey or bloated or weepy or forgetful or jittery—or all of the above—depending on which one I was taking. I was only *on* medication because of the labels—and like I said, the psychiatrist is the one who labels you.

I got labeled when I was in fourth grade. I'd been

digging through my mom's desk, looking for glue. Instead, I found something that looked like a test—except the questions weren't about math or history or science: they were about behavior.

The directions said to fill in the bubble that fit best. You had to pick whether the statements were not true, sometimes true, often true, or almost always true.

The child wanders aimlessly from one activity to another.
The child has difficulty relating to peers.
The child stares or gazes off into space.
The child gets teased a lot.
The child walks between two people who are talking.
The child offers comfort to others when they are sad.
The child has more difficulty with change than other children.

There were seventy-five statements. None of the bubbles had been filled in yet. My name was at the top of the page.

For a week, I snuck out of bed in the middle of the night to check the drawer and see if the bubbles had been filled in, bringing a notebook with me to write down the words I didn't know so I could look them up in the dictionary. I wanted to know if my mom thought that I never, sometimes, often, or almost always wander aimlessly from one activity to another. If she thought I never, sometimes, often, or almost always have difficulty relating to peers. If I never or always gaze off into space. If I never walk between two people who are talking. If I always get teased a lot.

If the child has more difficulty with change than other children.

I wanted to know what my mom thought of me. But I never found out because one night the bubbles were empty, and the next they were gone. They appeared again in the psychiatrist's office—but no one would show them to me. I remember that I was mad about the bubbles—and also mad because the psychiatrist said labels I didn't understand but looked up on the internet later, like "neurological disorder" and "attention deficit" and "poor executive functioning"— labels that were directed at me! There were all sorts of articles about how parents could "cope with" kids with these problems. Until the labels, I didn't know I was someone my mom had to "cope with." Until the labels, I didn't know I had "problems."

Mad about the bubbles and about not being included in the conversation and about being talked about in a way that felt gross, I had kicked the back of the psychiatrist's desk. That made my mom mad, which made me madder, which made me kick harder. Eventually, I melted out of the chair onto the floor, kicking the back of his desk with full force, over and over and over. My mom and the psychiatrist left until I calmed down, but before they did, I remember my mom crying. I don't like to think about that.

Sometimes I don't remember things at all, and sometimes I remember them too clearly. That's a thing I wish I'd forget.

"Frankie?" my mom asked, back in the present. She was holding a pile of my books and staring at me. I stared back at the reverse-parentheses wrinkles at the top of her nose between her eyebrows. "Did you hear me? I asked if I should call Gabe and make an appointment for you. I'm concerned that you haven't seen him in a while. And with everything going on now, I think it'd be a good idea."

Gabe is my therapist, which is way better than a psychiatrist. Therapists spend more time with you and try to talk to you and give you suggestions. I don't remember that much about the first time I met Gabe, but I do remember that his office was filled with board games and musical instruments and toys, and he talked to me alone, without my mom, and didn't label me or hide bubble worksheets from me. And he let me draw tornadoes while he asked me questions.

"Frankie, are you listening to me?" my mom asked.

"Yes!" I said, taking a deep breath. "But you don't need to call Gabe. I don't need to go to therapy every time some little thing happens." I focused on keeping my voice calm. "I'm fine. Don't worry."

Often, Gabe makes me feel better about things. But

I still didn't want to make an appointment with him. I wanted to prove that I could do it on my own. I didn't want weird Ms. Faust trying to smile at me at school. I wanted to be a normal person who could just live regularly without needing help every other minute.

And I was doing okay—as long as my routine stayed pretty much the same. But then Colette went missing—though I didn't know it was Colette for sure yet—and her current best friends, Tess and Mia, had asked me questions I hadn't exactly answered truthfully and I was home when I should have been in English, so my routine was not the same today.

My mom put down the books and moved super-close to the end of my bed, maybe going to sit on it, and I really didn't want her to. I have a thing about people sitting on my bed, even people I love like my mom.

"This isn't a little thing, Frankie . . ."

Don't sit on my bed, I thought.

"This is a big thing, a missing child."

Don't lean against it like that; it'll make you want to sit!

"Gabe might have some strategies for—"

She sat down.

"Mom! Stop!" I shouted at her, unable to keep my voice level anymore. "The kid is probably dead. We'll all just have to deal with it."

"Frances Vivienne Harper!" Mom gasped.

Whoops.

"I didn't mean that," I said quickly, backpedaling. "I just said that because I'm hungry."

"Get up, then," Mom said, mad, standing and turning toward the door, her knees popping when she moved. I don't know when she'd gotten so creaky. "We're going for a walk and then we'll eat. It's nonnegotiable." Her voice didn't have that nice mom tone to it anymore; it was flat.

"I don't want to go for a walk," I whined. "Can't we just eat lunch? I'm starving."

"You'll be fine," Mom said, still with an angry tone.

Tones are something therapists teach you to try to notice. Gabe calls them "cues." Most people just understand them automatically.

Thinking of that made me think of when I was little and I thought automatic toilets were called *automagic*. On my big list of things to do in life is to write a letter to the people who make the dictionary to see if they'll change it because my word is better. I was thinking about that when my mom raised her voice, which she rarely does.

"Frankie! Get up from that bed!"

"Fine," I said, knowing I was going to get in big trouble if I didn't.

When I stood up, she left. I pulled my puffy vest on over my hoodie, lifted the hood over my head. I couldn't remember when I'd last brushed my hair and there was a huge nest in it. I like my hair—it's really thick and wavy—but I don't like brushing out the nests it makes at all.

I stepped into my red rain boots and tromped out of my room, down the hall, and to the elevator. My mom says the elevators are for the guests—did I mention that we live in an inn?—but I felt like breaking the rules.

Outside, the billowy clouds had parted, and I could see blue sky for miles. It was windy, so I kept my hood up over my head. Wind in my ears is terrible.

Charles, my mom's boyfriend, and our dog, Pirate, were waiting for me in the parking lot, ready to go for a walk on the beach. Charles had on his usual outdoor uniform: work boots, faded jeans, a black T-shirt, a gray windbreaker, and a red beanie with his light brown hair flipping out underneath. When it wasn't topped with a beanie, Charles wore his hair messy, like I did, but his was styled to look that way—with special organic hair products he ordered from Seattle and that my mom teased him about, which usually made him kiss her, which always grossed me out.

I like Charles and used to wonder sometimes if my mom would marry him, but then she didn't so I stopped wondering. My mom isn't the marrying kind: she and my biological father weren't married. Well, I mean, he was married . . . but to someone else. Adults make dumb choices sometimes, but I guess if they hadn't made that dumb choice, I wouldn't exist.

Anyway, my mom and Charles work a lot, so they started this tradition of meeting up at break times for a short walk. Usually, we only have to do it on weekends or when we're off school for teacher work days. I guess they didn't feel like they were seeing me or my sister enough—or asking us enough uncomfortable questions.

"Hey, boss," Charles said, holding out a to-go cup that I knew had hot chocolate in it. His jacket sleeve pulled back when he reached out, showing a peek of the tattoos that covered his entire arm. Arms.

I grunted something as I accepted the cup.

"Say it's mint tea if she asks," Charles instructed, scratching his stubble, and I nodded. My mom doesn't want us having sugar all the time. Well, she doesn't want *me* having it all the time. Or red dye. Or processed foods. "You okay?"

"I'm okay," I said, giving Pirate a rub behind her ear. Her name is Pirate because another dog scratched out her left eye in a fight and she looks like she has a permanent eye patch. It's pretty disgusting, but the rest of her is cute so I try not to look at her eye and love her anyway.

"Did they leave without us?"

"I told them to go ahead," Charles said. "I said we'd catch up."

Charles looked at me sideways like he was trying to figure out my mood, which he does a lot. Sometimes I'm okay with it and sometimes I want to growl at him, which I don't do anymore because Gabe says it's socially unacceptable, but I still think it's a useful way of telling someone to quit it.

It's hard to understand why expressing yourself in growls or just directly saying that you don't like something is bad. Manners seem like wrapping words in cotton balls, and I think it's just easier to say the words without the fluff. I don't have any friends, though, so I'm probably wrong. You probably shouldn't take any of my advice.

We started walking and we didn't say any words for a while—regular ones or cotton-ball ones. The silence made me happy. I missed that about being friends with Colette: she was good at walking without talking without it being weird.

I listened to the sound of Pirate's tags clanking together as we went down the short paved road toward the ocean. They made a little song and I imagined myself dancing, but didn't actually do it.

Soon the pavement turned to sand and my bootheels dug in deeper with every step. I splashed through puddles from a quick rain that had happened earlier, then moved over to the left side of the sandy path to run my hand along the wispy beach grass that came up to my waist.

We got to the point where the grass ends and opens up to the beach, which stretches for miles in both directions. I shaded my eyes so I could see where my mom was: she and my sister were walking at the edge of the tide.

"Some people think the missing kid might be Colette,"

I said to Charles, watching the water. It was choppy today and looked like the waves were siblings fighting with each other. The wind was threatening to pull back my hood, so I yanked the strings tighter. "She wasn't at school today and no one could reach her."

"It's scary, no matter who it is," Charles said.

"Yeah," I said, not sure I really felt scared. I felt more like a mixture of curious and excited, which I'm pretty sure is not the right way to feel when a kid from your school could be in trouble. My emotions don't always work like they're supposed to, and it felt like they were extra off right then because I should have been at school, but I was walking on the beach.

"What if they don't find the kid?" I asked Charles, watching my mom and sister walking, holding hands. I didn't do that with my mom, and it made me feel jealous.

"That would be awful," Charles said, taking Pirate off her leash. She bolted toward the water to chase the seagulls as they searched for lunch of their own. "No matter who it is, it'd be awful."

"Yeah," I said, wondering if I'd really feel awful or if I'd have to pretend to feel awful so everyone wouldn't think I was weird.

Pirate bounded back our way with a huge stick in her mouth, circled Charles, and dropped it near his feet. She waited for him to throw it, then took off again in a flash.

"Hey, Charles?"

"Yeah?"

"I think it's Colette," I said. I just had a feeling.

The truth was, I'd lied to Tess and Mia: I *had* seen Colette the day before. She'd randomly come by my room for the first time since February. We'd had a fight and she'd left. Thinking through the fight was the reason I couldn't fall asleep the night before: it'd stuck with me into the late-night hours. Now I was feeling really confused.

"I hope you're wrong, buddy," Charles said, smiling at me.

Me too, I thought.

"Now what's she doing?" Charles asked, shielding his eyes from the sun and watching Pirate. It looked like she was trying to dig up a crab. "She's going to get pinched again," he said. "I'll be right back."

I nodded and walked over to a log that the ocean hadn't wanted anymore. It had sand packed into the grooves, but it was dry enough to use as a bench. I inspected it for bugs, then sat down, thinking about nothing or everything.

I picked up a stick and wrote *Hi* in the wet sand.

Charles took the stick and wrote in the sand *Hi back.* I hadn't noticed him there again. Then my mom and sister were on their way toward us, and I wondered how much time had gone by while I was spacing out. That happens sometimes.

"What's in the cup?" Mom asked.

"Hot chocolate," I said without thinking. My mom gave Charles a mad-ish look and Charles shrugged.

"No more sugar for you today," Mom said to me, continuing on toward the inn. Charles and Pirate started jogging together in the same direction.

My sister followed them, and as she walked by me, she said, "That sucks for you. She just said she's making chocolate cake for dessert tonight."

"Why are you always so annoying?" I snapped. It was only when I saw the hurt in her eyes that I realized she'd been showing empathy, not rubbing it in.

"Whatever, Frankie," Tess said quietly, shaking her head. "I don't know what's going on with you lately."

She ran off like a gazelle on her long legs and I was left to walk back to the inn alone on my shorter ones.

Oh, did I say that Tess is my sister? Yeah, she is. She's one minute older than me. Yes, that means we're twins. Not identical ones: the fraternal kind.

And yes, my twin sister stole the only friend I'd ever had.

chapter 3

Myth: Tornadoes bring a drop in atmospheric
pressure that will make your house explode
if your house is closed up.

MY MOM AND Charles live in a cottage behind the inn. Tess and I shared the second bedroom in the cottage until we started middle school. That's when Tess asked Mom if it'd be okay if she started using one of the rooms inside the inn, one of the ones that didn't have a view or anything.

Tess had explained that all of her friends had their own rooms and she needed privacy to work on her art. She wanted to go to art school someday, which I bet she could, except then she'd have to show her drawings to someone and that freaks her out for some reason so maybe not. Anyway, when Tess asked for her own room, I didn't think it was about art: I thought it was about not wanting to share a room with me anymore.

Whatever the reason, Mom and Charles agreed. Mom

set ground rules for Tess, like she could never let anyone in her room without getting permission, and she always had to keep the door bolted at night, and she had to be in her room at nine and stay there all night, and she had to check in with Mom or Charles before going to sleep.

Then I told them that it wasn't fair that Tess got to have a room at the inn and I didn't. Mom probably felt more nervous about letting me do it than Tess—because she trusts Tess more than she trusts me—but she said yes. She made us have connecting rooms, which, honestly, made me feel a lot better because I wasn't sure I'd wanted to move out of the cottage. The whole first year, Tess and I slept with the doors connecting our rooms wide open. Did you know some people think your house will explode if your windows and doors are shut during a tornado? It's not true, but I liked the doors open anyway. Except at the beginning of this school year, Tess started closing hers. And it was weird to have hers closed and mine open, so I started closing mine, too.

I was thinking about how I didn't like closed doors while I watched Tess texting. She had her knees pulled up into the chair and the light from the screen was making her skin look blue. Her thumbs went *tap-tap-tap-tap*, then she waited, biting her thumbnail, for a response.

"Who are you texting?" I asked.

Tess looked up at me sharply, then at Mom's back. Mom

was over by the sink cutting cucumbers into slices for the guest water jugs. The water was running so she hadn't heard me.

"It's a group text," Tess whispered. "Everyone's wondering who the kid is that's missing. Some people got called to the police station."

The water turned off. "Who's in the group text?" I asked.

Mom turned around quickly. "Tess!" she said. "No phones at the table, you know the rule—especially right now, with everything that's going on." She walked over and held out a wet hand for the phone.

Tess frowned at me and handed it over. "Sorry, Mom."

I watched Tess dunk her grilled cheese in her tomato soup and take a bite. She did it so perfectly, not dripping any soup from the bowl to her mouth. My whole body felt aware of the fact that we were at the cottage instead of the cafeteria. I didn't like the alteration in my normal schedule.

"Do you have homework?" Mom asked, not directing the question at either of us. I thought it was weird she was asking about homework, but parents are weird sometimes.

"We didn't have school except for part of first period," I said to her back, leaving a trail of tomato soup like a crime scene on the tablecloth. "How could we have homework?"

"I'm going to work on my portfolio this afternoon," Tess said, probably just to make herself look good since she was mad at me for getting her phone taken away.

"Good for you," I grumbled. Mom turned around and gave me a sharp look.

"Be kind to your sister," she said. "And you'd be smart to work on your big science project. That's a great thing to do today. It'd be a nice distraction."

"That's what I was thinking," Tess said.

"It's not due until May," I protested.

"Yes, but May is only two weeks away, and it's a big undertaking," Mom said. "It'll mean a lot of planning and organization. And you'll want to write and rewrite your assessment to make sure it says exactly what you want it to say." I didn't answer her, because I probably wasn't going to do that and we both knew it, so she asked, "Well, what are you going to do today, then? I want you to find something *productive*. You can't just wander around aimlessly or watch *Tornado Alley* all day."

I rolled my eyes. "Mom, it's *Tornado Ally*. Geez."

"Whatever it's called, you can't spend your whole day watching it," she replied as my brain wandered off.

I'd been watching *Tornado Ally* when Colette knocked on my door the night before. I ignored the first knocks. And the second set. I thought it was a guest knocking on the wrong door, which happens more than you might think. But after the third set of knocks, I flung open the door impatiently.

"Hi, Frankie," Colette said like it was nothing, like she hadn't ignored me since February. She had her bright red hair pulled back in a knot and a big smile on her super-freckled face. She was wearing a blue sweatshirt with a dolphin pattern. The sweatshirt was a little too tight in the waist.

"Hi," I said, going back to my desk.

"I see you're busy," she said, barely stepping into the room. She knew I didn't like people in my space. "I won't stay long, but I was wondering if I could borrow that old notebook? That we used to write in?" I turned in my chair and gave her an annoyed look. She pulled down the hem of her sweatshirt and explained: "I want to copy something."

"No," I said, flipping around to face my computer.

"No?" Colette asked, like she couldn't believe I wouldn't just hand over what she wanted after she hadn't spoken to me for two months.

"No," I said. "You can't have it."

"Come on, Frankie," she said. "I'll take care of it and I'll bring it back. I'll give it to you at school tomorrow."

"No!" I said forcefully, staring at the screen. I could see her reflection in it.

I heard her take a deep breath behind me. "Are you going to do homework at your mom's cottage?"

"None of your business," I said. *Why do you care about my homework?*

"Will you just let me borrow the notebook, please?" Colette asked, sweetness in her voice.

"No!" I shouted.

"Why not?" Colette demanded, anger replacing the sweetness. "It's mine as much as it's yours."

"I lost it," I said quietly, tapping my fingernail on the mouse too softly to make it actually go *click*. My cheeks were growing hot.

"I can tell you're lying," Colette said. "You never look at me when you lie. Why do you have to be like that?"

The little monsters inside that turn up my temperature and make me scream were gathering—and I told myself with my voice on zero that yelling at Colette wouldn't be a good idea because my mom might hear. Or a guest might call the front desk and tell her. Instead, I grabbed my noise-canceling headphones and put them on.

A few seconds later, I felt the door shut hard. It wasn't a slam because Colette wouldn't do that. Only I slam doors, it seems—

"Frankie!" Mom said urgently, pulling me out of my memory. "Please listen to me."

"What?" I asked, blinking, no clue how long she'd been talking to me. "What's happening?"

Tess sighed.

"What?"

She shook her head at me.

"I just got off the phone with the police," Mom said. I hadn't heard her phone ring—I hadn't heard her talking.

I was wondering if my ears were working properly when my mom said, "I'm so sorry, girls, but they told me that the missing girl *is* Colette."

"I knew it," I said flatly.

"No!" Tess wailed over my words, like she hadn't already thought the same thing, tears rushing down her face. "Where do they think she is? Have they checked hospitals? This can't be happening!"

"They don't know anything," Mom said, hugging Tess. She smoothed her hair and wiped her cheeks. "They're trying their hardest to find her. That's why they want her friends to come in and answer some questions. They're hoping it might help."

"When?" Tess whispered.

"Right now."

chapter 4

Fact: Sometimes you can't see a tornado.

MY SISTER AND I stopped having joint birthday parties when we were eleven.

Even though she's not that outgoing, everyone likes Tess. It seems like because she doesn't try to be everyone's friend, they all try harder to be hers. And when it came to our birthday parties, Tess always invited the whole class so no one would feel left out.

Often there would be a theme, like princess or circus or like when we turned eight and my mom let us have Halloween in August. That was Tess's favorite because she loves anything scary and she and Charles made a kid-friendly haunted house in the inn's function room. I hated it. There was this part of the party where Charles, dressed like a zombie, hid behind a door and jumped out when kids came in. It'd made Tess practically pee her pants with laughter, but I'd burst into tears.

Anyway, the parties came with a lot of squealing and stampeding—even from quiet Tess—and usually made me feel like I was watching a noisy kaleidoscope from the corner of a room, depending on which medication they were giving me then.

Medication for someone like me isn't easy. My "challenges," as Gabe calls them, are invisible—just like tornadoes you can't see until they wipe out people's houses in the middle of the night. My mom says my brain is special, but the psychiatrist will tell you that I have several neurological conditions: attention deficit disorder, Asperger's syndrome, and sensory processing disorder. And they aren't as simple as having strep throat and getting antibiotics to treat it. That's why, after the labels, the psychiatrist experimented on me with a bunch of stuff. But nothing ever felt right, and even on medication, I still felt like screaming and crying and generally melting down a lot of the time. Definitely at my birthday parties.

So I stopped having parties. That's why my eleventh birthday was the best one ever.

"If you're not going to have a party, what would you like to do to celebrate your birthday?" my mom asked. "You're turning eleven! And you've had such a great year. There's a lot to celebrate."

It was a Saturday morning and we were all hanging out in the living room of the cottage. Tess was curled up sideways in the big chair, a horror book in front of her face, not really paying attention. Charles wrestled Pirate on the floor, getting dog hair all over his T-shirt for some old rock band I'd never heard of, and Mom and I were on opposite ends of the couch kind of watching whatever movie was playing on whatever channel the TV was on. Everyone was wearing pajama bottoms.

I tossed a pillow in the air and caught it, over and over. I was literally throwing a throw pillow.

"Maybe we could go to the arcade," I said.

Toss. Catch. Toss. Catch. Toss. Catch.

"Okay," Mom said enthusiastically. "We could—"

"Never mind," I interrupted, not wanting her to turn it into a big thing. *Toss. Catch.* "I don't want to go there." I thought a little more, liking the control of planning my very own non-party. "Can I sleep in a tent on the beach?"

Toss. Catch. Toss. Catch.

"Since the beach is technically a road, you can't do that, unfortunately," Charles answered, looking up at me from the floor with his smiling eyes and humongous wild eyebrows. "Sleeping on a road isn't a great idea."

"Ha," I said—not laughing, just saying it—tossing the pillow again. "Can I at least have a fire?"

"Sure," Mom said. I glanced at her and she was watching

me toss the pillow with an expression like that emoji with the perfectly straight mouth, like she wanted to tell me to stop, but knew it would be better not to. Instead, she said, "We can make dinner and s'mores. It'll be great! I could make skewers. You like skewers!" She smiled then; she looked better when she smiled.

"Okay, but I was thinking it'd be a smaller number of people," I said, focusing on the pillow because I knew my mom was going to make a sad-emoji face, and I knew I wouldn't like it. "I just wanted to invite Colette."

"You're not inviting your sister?" Mom asked.

"Are you coming to my party?" Tess asked in a low voice. I guess she had been paying attention after all. I don't know; maybe she always is and just pretends not to be.

"No," I said quickly. Mom was planning to drive Tess and eight friends all the way to Aberdeen to go roller skating, which sounded horrible for at least seven reasons.

"Sorry, Mom, but Frankie's right. It's only fair that I don't go to hers if she's not going to mine," Tess said matter-of-factly.

"But that's . . . ," Mom said, her voice fading away. "You've always . . ." Her voice faded again. She cleared her throat. "The two of you and Colette play together all the time. Are you sure this won't be . . . weird?"

"We don't *play* together," Tess said, her cheeks pink. "We hang out. And it's fine, Mom, really." I think she understood that I placed a lot of value in fairness—and if I wasn't going to her party, then she wasn't going to mine. Fair is fair.

"Well, I'll do something with Tess, then," Mom said. "But you can't light a fire on your own, Frankie. Charles will have to go with you. Or I could, and Tess and Charles could do something?"

"Um . . . ," I said, not hiding a smile. My mom is the worst at starting fires.

"I get it," she said, laughing. "Charles is in charge of the fire."

"That's fine," I said, meaning it. Charles may have been a lawyer before he moved to Long Beach, but he didn't act like it—he acted like a mature kid—so I knew he'd be okay to have around.

On the evening of my non-party, which was the first Saturday after my actual eleventh birthday, Colette, Charles, and I loaded up one of the inn's wagons with firewood, kindling, a lighter, beach blankets, beach chairs, hot dogs, sodas, and stuff to make s'mores. Charles pulled the wagon ahead of us with Pirate circling him like a maniac, seeming as excited to be going to the beach as I was.

We meandered to the right side of the sand path and walked in a line so we could touch the tall beach grass as we went. This car entrance to the beach was closed to protect the razor clam beds from getting crushed. It was illegal to drive onto the beach this way during clam season or

47

to ride a horse over this section of the beach this time of year. Charles was extreme: he wouldn't even let us ride *bikes* through the entrance. Since cars had to drive onto the beach from the north or south entrances, the usual deep tire tracks were filled in by thick, tiny mountains of dry sand.

"What did you do today?" Colette asked.

"I don't know," I said with a shrug. "Nothing."

"Oh," Colette said. "My mom made me go to the grocery store with her and then she took me to the library and I got the next graphic novel in that series I like and then we got smoothies." She paused for a breath. "If you could only have mango or strawberry smoothies for the rest of your life, what would you pick?"

"Mango."

"You didn't think about that very long."

"I hate strawberries."

"If you had to eat strawberries or broccoli for dinner, which one would you choose?" she asked.

"I'd skip dinner," I said, brushing the hair out of my mouth. Colette had her hair pulled up in knots like Mickey Mouse ears, and I maybe should have pulled mine back, too, to keep it out of my mouth, but I hate the feeling of having my ears exposed. And I can't put a hoodie over a ponytail or knot. And hair bands give me headaches.

We'd made it to the medium-dry sand then. I loved looking at the different tracks made by toes and shoe treads and webbed feet and paws, leading around in circles or swirls, a giant game of connect-the-dots between pieces of washed-up seaweed, logs, and shells. I kicked an empty crab claw.

"I brought you a present," Colette said, pausing to take off her flip-flops. "I also brought some music so we can sing if we want to, and two new quiz books."

"I love quizzes," I said. I don't love singing, but I didn't say that.

"I know. This is going to be so fun! My mom said your mom said we could stay out here until ten!"

"I know!" I said, looking toward the water. "It's the best!"

The beach made me feel calm. The tide was low, and the sand near the water was rippled from the waves rolling in and out when the tide had been higher. My eyes got stuck until Colette spoke again.

"What's Tess doing tonight?"

"She went to a movie with our mom," I said flatly. I didn't want her to ask about Tess. Maybe she got that, because she started to run toward where Charles had stopped the wagon and was unloading supplies.

"Let's go!" Colette shouted over her shoulder. Sinking deep into the sand, she looked like she was running in slow motion. Her cheeks were extra pink and her blue eyes were really bright. "It's time to build the fire!"

Just before the sun disappeared that night, Charles used my first phone to take a picture of Colette and me at the water's edge. In the picture, the sky is light blue and periwinkle at the top. The clouds are gray at the bottom, but coral and gold tipped because of the way the sun's rays are hitting them. Colette and I are silhouettes: one with blowing hair and the other with Mickey Mouse ears. The glassy wet sand reflects the sky and our shadows; we're laughing, the legs of our pants wet from not running fast enough when the waves came in.

That picture of me and Colette at sunset is my favorite picture ever.

I don't have it anymore.

———

THE LONG BEACH Police Station is a squat little box covered entirely in wood shingles, not just on the roof. The worn pieces of wood are nailed in rows on top of rows and faded from the sun—and they look like they'd give you splinters if you ran your hand along them.

The clock on the post cemented to the sidewalk in front of the station said one forty-five, except that it was only one fifteen. I should have been starting my weekend after my early-release morning, but I was here, at the police station.

The clock had been stuck on one forty-five since last summer. It drove me crazy that they didn't fix it. That's an example of how I notice things too much—I couldn't *not* notice, and be bugged by, the stupid clock. It was like a mental hangnail. I think I might get those more than other people, like Tess. She wasn't bugged by the clock.

"Why won't they fix that thing already?" I asked no one in particular.

"Sorry, but how can you be talking about the clock right now when Colette is missing?" Tess asked softly, pulling her sweater tighter around her.

"I'm just saying they should fix it."

Mom held open the door to the police station and I was glad because I didn't want to touch it. I walked through, still stuck on the clock. "It makes no sense that they don't. People need to know what time it is. The *police* need to know what time it is!"

Tess had stopped listening to me.

There were five kids sitting in the chairs lining the wall by the front desk, all of them with one or both parents, except the parents were all sitting in chairs on the opposite wall.

Mia ran over and hugged Tess; she'd saved her a seat. Colette's weird neighbor, Naomi, smiled and waved like she was at some great social event, not about to be questioned by the police. Bryce and Colin were there, of course, since a couple months ago, Colette and Bryce had declared themselves boyfriend-girlfriend and Colin is Bryce's best friend.

People had started calling Colette and Bryce *Brolette*, which is so weird. And it'd been especially weird since

Colette and Bryce had barely ever talked to each other before they'd decided to become a name mash-up.

Sitting next to Colin at the station, on the edge of his chair with his skateboard between his knees, was . . . Kai?

"What are *you* doing here?" I asked before I could get control of the wild horses that sometimes race out of my mouth.

"I . . . uh . . . ," Kai answered, glancing down at the NO HATE JUST SKATE sticker on the top of his board. He looked back at me with his super-dark brown eyes and shrugged.

I resisted a compulsive need to try to touch the tips of his blown-forward black hair or soft-looking skin. I really don't like when people touch me, but when I want to touch things, it's almost painful if I can't.

"That wasn't very nice," my mom whispered harshly as she nudged me toward two open seats on the parent side. I pulled away from her breath in my ear.

"Stop it," I said loudly.

Mom looked embarrassed, but I didn't care much because I was preoccupied by wishing she didn't feel like she had to remind me every time I made a mistake—I almost always already knew—and being mad that she'd whispered in my ear because she should know by now that whispers feel absolutely terrible to me.

I had my finger in my ear, trying to make it feel better,

when two policemen came out and talked to us. I knew one of them: it was Maggie Saunders's dad. He'd spoken at Career Day in fourth grade. He had a round face with an extra chin or two, and I liked him because one time, when he'd caught me cry-laughing while hugging a headstone in the cemetery, he said he wouldn't tell my parents if I promised not to do it again.

I'd never seen the one who wasn't Mr. Saunders before, and he was exactly the opposite of Mr. Saunders. He had humongous muscles and had one of those beard things that wraps all the way around your mouth. I could tell that he was definitely in charge. His name tag said ROLLINS.

"Mia Gilmore?" Officer Rollins asked, and Mia jumped a little. She gave my sister another hug, because they can't do anything without hugging first, which makes me cringe, and then Mia and her mom followed the officers away from our group.

Colin started telling Tess about getting his braces tightened, and Kai answered a question from Naomi about homework, messing with the corner of a sticker on his board deck that was coming up while he talked. When I looked at Bryce, he was staring into space with his light blue eyes. Bryce had never seemed that interesting to me and, as I stared at him staring at nothing, I couldn't understand why Colette would want to pick him to be her first boyfriend.

I wondered if they'd kissed. The thought of kissing a boy completely freaked me out because, I can't be positive, but I'm pretty sure that means someone would touch you.

I don't know why I looked at Kai again right then, but I did. Now he was hunched over, typing on his phone, his mouth open a little in concentration. That's how he sometimes looks when he takes tests, too. Before he caught me watching him, I pulled out my own phone and started reading the latest post on my favorite blog, written by a famous tornado chaser.

Kids and their parents went in, stayed awhile, and left. The police didn't take more than fifteen minutes with each kid, but it felt like forever. Mom went in with Tess and when they came out, Tess's eyes were red and puffy. Tess begged Mom to let her leave without us so she could go to Mia's house and Mom agreed. Finally when I was the last kid in the waiting room, Officer Rollins called my name. My mom and I followed him toward an interview room, but she asked me to wait outside for a few seconds.

"May I speak with you privately first?" Mom asked the officer.

"Of course," he said, and they left me leaning against the wall, listening through a crack in the door.

"I wanted to let you know that Frankie's not neurotypical," my mom began quietly. "She may not answer questions logically or may interrupt when you're speaking. She's very impulsive and she doesn't react well to change, so it's more challenging for her to be here than the other kids. Also, she has SPD, which means that she's very sensitive to touch and may have a big reaction if—"

I tuned out, my cheeks red with embarrassment.

I don't know why I'm the only one whose mom has to warn people in advance.

chapter 5

Fact: The part of the United States
that gets the most destructive tornadoes
is called Tornado Alley.

"HAVE A SEAT, Frances," Officer Rollins said when it was finally my turn in the interview room. My mom sat in the chair closest to the wall. She pulled her frumpy sweatshirt tight around her like she was freezing, but it was hot in the room.

"I wanted to sit there," I said to her, crossing my arms over my chest.

"Be flexible, please," she said.

"I am," I said. "I'm trying." Flexibility is a big deal to her. And to therapists. And, I guess, to people in general. "But can I sit there?"

My mom sighed and moved to the other chair. I bumped her knee and stepped on her toe trying to get around her to sit down in the chair by the wall. "It's too warm," I grumbled, but I stayed put.

"Shall we get started, Frances?" Officer Rollins asked from across the wooden table.

"My name's Frankie," I said, shifting in the hard-back chair with the warm seat. I wished I was at the beach. That's what probably made me ask, "Are you from Long Beach?"

He shook his head. "Tacoma."

"I like Wild Waves," I said.

"Wild Waves is in Federal Way," Officer Rollins said.

"Isn't that close to Tacoma?" I asked. "Like right next to it? Like basically part of it?" He shrugged so I tried again. "I also like the Tacoma zoo."

"Most people do."

"You don't?"

"Well, I'm a grown-up." I thought he was going to give more explanation, so I waited, but he didn't.

"Grown-ups can like zoos."

"Frankie, will you let the man speak?" Mom interrupted. She'd scooted her chair back a little so she was halfway behind me.

I turned around to look at her. "You're creeping me out. Move your chair back up the way it was."

"Don't be bossy," Mom said. "And please remember that Officer Rollins is in charge of this conversation, not you."

"I know he is," I said to my mom. I hoped that she wasn't making a mental list of all the ways I was *not* doing great today—all the reasons to make me start taking medication again. Or at least force me to go talk to Gabe.

She moved her chair forward so she was next to me.

I scanned the corners of the room where the walls met the ceiling. "Is this being recorded?"

My mom sighed.

"Yes," Officer Rollins said.

"Where's the camera?" I asked. My mom cleared her throat, probably trying to remind me to let Officer Rollins talk.

Okay, yes, I talk a lot. Gabe sometimes reminds me not to "monopolize the conversation," which apparently means talking about what you want to talk about and not pausing to listen to what other people want to say—even if you think what they want to say is boring or annoying. It doesn't matter: you still have to do it.

Officer Rollins had his superhuman forearms on the table, and he raised his right one like a drawbridge, pointing up, showing me where the camera was mounted.

"I see it," I said, craning my neck to look at the little dome near the overhead light with a tiny red eye peeking out. "Thanks. That would have bugged me."

"What would have?" Officer Rollins asked, stroking his face fur.

"Looking for the camera," I said. "Better I just know where it is to begin with."

The right corner of Officer Rollins's mouth lifted like it was considering going full-smile but then got tired and defaulted to a frown. His circle beard made it look like he was stuck that way.

I wondered whether he was able to smile. *Is there something wrong with your face? Smiling isn't necessary all the time. Clowns smile too much . . . They're so creepy. Creepy like the Sea Witch. Remember that time we—*

"Is it okay if I ask *you* some questions now?" Officer Rollins asked, interrupting my winding train of thought. I nodded even though, let's be honest, I wanted to ask more about the camera if we were going to talk about anything. "I'll start by saying that you're not in any trouble."

"Why would I be in trouble? Colette's the one missing."

"Yes," he said, smiling for real that time. "And we're trying to find her, which is why we asked all of you in today— to see if you can give us any clues that will help us do that."

"Did you check her phone?" I asked. "Her whole life is on her phone."

"We assume she has her phone with her," Officer Rollins said. "But her phone is off, so we haven't been able to pinpoint her location."

"How about her computer?" I asked. He sighed, and I said, "Okay, you ask the questions."

"Thanks." He checked something in a tan leather notebook in front of him. "So you're one of Colette's best friends, is that right?"

"No."

"No? That's what the other kids said."

My mom shifted in her chair.

"Well, I *used* to be friends with Colette," I clarified, "but we're not friends anymore." Officer Rollins looked at me like he wanted more of an explanation than that, so I kept talking. "When we were younger, Colette and I were best friends . . . and my sister and Colette were friends, too. The three of us hung out together a lot. Then Mia moved here in middle school and joined our group and Tess and Colette both really liked her but I didn't, and then the group changed and I was . . ." I thought about that a second, not knowing what to say. Feeling silly about saying the truth, that I was left behind. "We just stopped being friends. That's all."

Officer Rollins nodded and said, "I get it. I have a fifteen-year-old daughter."

"I'm thirteen."

"I know," he said, smiling. "I'm just saying that I know how these things go."

While he made notes, I noticed that there wasn't a clock in the room. I wondered if that was on purpose, like an interrogation tactic for criminals or something. The room didn't seem very menacing, though: I mean, there was a poster of the beach at sunset.

I daydreamed about building sandcastles with Colette and Tess, racing to stack packed sand bricks as high as we could before the tide came in and swept them away.

"Frankie?" Officer Rollins asked.

"What?" I tuned back in to the conversation. I guess he'd been having it without me.

"I asked: When you were friends, what did Colette like to do?"

"Sing," I answered.

"Oh yeah?"

I nodded. "She secretly wants to be a pop star. She writes songs all the time—or at least she used to." I looked at my mom. "Her parents don't know that, so don't tell them."

Mom smiled at me, and I looked back at Officer Rollins, adding, "She's a pretty good singer."

"That's great information, Frankie. No one else told us that Colette likes to sing." I couldn't help it; I smiled at the praise. He continued, "Do you think that Colette ran away?"

I laughed out loud. "No!" I said. "She's only thirteen! And she's not that brave." Colette couldn't even hug a tombstone.

"But do you think it's *possible* that she ran away? Even remotely?" he asked, looking up at me from his super-messy handwriting. There was no way I could read what it said upside down.

"No," I said. I felt antsy and started swinging my feet.

"We're almost finished," Officer Rollins said, looking down at my feet. He used the end of his pen to skim through his notes. "Just one last question and then you can go, Frankie."

"Okay," I said, glancing at my mom. She gave me an encouraging smile that made me feel like I'd done a reasonable job answering the questions. Then I got the one I didn't want to hear.

"When's the last time you saw Colette?"

No!

I'd decided that lying to the police would be a very bad idea. I'd made a deal with myself that if they asked directly, I'd tell the truth. But now Officer Rollins was looking at me with a question-mark face and it made me really nervous because right after the last time I'd seen Colette, she'd disappeared. And I didn't like feeling like it was even a little bit my fault. Because it absolutely, positively wasn't.

"I saw Colette last night," I blurted out, making Officer Rollins look up at me, surprised.

"What?" my mom said, sitting straighter in her chair. "Why didn't you say anything abou—"

"If you could let Frankie speak, please," Officer Rollins interrupted.

"Sorry," Mom said, "go ahead, Frankie."

"She came to my room at six forty-five."

"I see, and . . . ," Officer Rollins began. Then his words faded and his forehead wrinkled up in confusion. He flipped quickly through the pages in his notebook to find a certain entry. "Do you mean six forty-five in the morning yesterday?"

"Uh . . . no," I said, laughing. "Who would come over that early?"

"You're saying that Colette came to your room at six forty-five in the evening *yesterday*?" I nodded, and he looked at me sternly. "How do you know what time it was?"

"It was right in the middle of *Tornado Ally* and I was annoyed that she was making me miss watching it live." He didn't say anything, so I added, "I don't like watching it recorded and Colette knows that. And it was getting close to homework time, and I'd have to stop watching and leave my room, which made it doubly annoying."

"Why did you have to leave your room to do homework?" Officer Rollins asked. "Did you go to the library?"

I gave my mom a look. "*She* makes me do it at the cottage so she can watch me."

"So I can *help* you," Mom said quietly.

Officer Rollins rubbed his eyes with the palms of his hands and then rubbed his forehead and bald head and I wondered if he'd stop before rubbing his skin off but then he finally stopped. "Frankie, is this some kind of a joke?" he asked.

"What are you talking about?" I asked, not seeing the humor in it at all. I stared at him seriously. Then I got distracted by the number of lines on his forehead. I started counting them: *one, two, three, four . . .*

"Frankie?" He'd raised his eyebrows, making the lines really pronounced. He looked at my mom with an expression that I interpreted as: *I see what you mean.*

I wanted to act normal, but I didn't know what he'd said. "Huh?"

"Will you please try to pay attention?" my mom asked.

"I am!" I snapped.

Officer Rollins took a deep breath. "Frankie, I was saying that someone else said that Colette visited them at precisely six forty-five last evening and stayed for about twenty minutes, and unless Colette is magic, I don't think she could have been in two places at once."

"She's not magic," I said, confused, "and I'm not lying. I know when *Tornado Ally* was posted—you can check on Viewer."

"I'm sorry, are you saying tornado *ally,* or *alley*?" Officer Rollins asked.

"*Ally*, just like I said," I answered. "Like a friend of tornadoes, not Tornado Alley, the place that gets the most tornadoes in the country." I rolled my eyes. "Although all these questions are making me feel like I'm in Tornado Alley . . . and like I need an ally," I joked. No one laughed. I was embarrassed. "I'm telling the truth about when Colette came to my room, too. She was there for like ten minutes. Or fifteen, maybe. The other person has to be lying."

Was it ten? Or more like five? I had no idea, but I wasn't telling him that.

"And you're sure it wasn't more like six thirty when she came by? Because then she could have made it—"

"I'm one hundred percent sure," I interrupted him.

My mom cleared her throat again.

"I wonder if you'd say that if you knew who it was," Officer Rollins said.

"Who is it?" My head was spinning. I was *positive* I'd told him the right time. Why would someone else say Colette had visited them then, too? They were clearly lying! "Tell me who said that."

Officer Rollins closed his notebook and frowned at me. Both adults were quiet for a long time, looking at each other, then at me, then back at each other. Finally my mom shrugged, and Officer Rollins answered the question.

"It was Tess."

chapter 6

Fact: The majority of tornadoes
only last for a few minutes.

I PUSHED THROUGH the doors of the police station and paused on the sidewalk, my hands balled into fists. A female officer was going into the building, carrying a big envelope, and she almost ran into me. I didn't apologize for stopping abruptly in her path because I was fighting back angry tears. And I was in the worst possible place to cry: right on Pacific Avenue. In a story about our town, Pacific Avenue would have been called Main Street.

My mom had stayed behind to speak with the officer again privately, frustrating me even more. I turned left and walked past the mini-carnival, closed until Memorial Day, to the benches by the fourteen-foot-tall frying pan. The sign in front of the frying pan will tell you it's from the

1940s and was put there in celebration of the clam festival. I sat down and avoided looking at the tourists getting their pictures taken while pretending to be bacon, which is the least original idea ever.

I tried to talk myself down from ten, because if my mom came out and saw me losing it, that would go on her list of reasons why I should be on medication.

Colette is probably perfectly fine and she'll be home soon, I told myself. *We will all go back to school on Monday and have our normal day and this will just be a weird thing that happened.*

That's self-talk. It's supposed to help, but it didn't. I kicked my heel against the bench a few times, grunting. My face probably looked mad, because when the tourists at the frying pan noticed me, they walked away.

Stop it! I told myself. *Mom's coming out soon.*

I forced myself to stop kicking the bench. I forced my mouth into a fake smile, because sometimes if you do that, you'll accidentally really smile. I didn't, but maybe a weird fake smile looked better than a scowl. I focused on uncurling my fists. Finally I flipped my hands over so my palms were facing up. Someone had told me to do that once—and today, that was the thing that worked. The cool breeze on my palms felt so nice and calming that my fake smile faded to a neutral face and I didn't have to think so much about not kicking the bench: I just didn't do it.

I sniffed and checked my phone. It was 2:50 in the afternoon. Even though it'd felt like longer, my internal freakout had only lasted a few minutes.

I looked across the street at Marsh's Free Museum, which is more of a curiosity gift shop than a museum so I'm not sure why it's called that. The parking lot was crowded because it was starting to get warmer since it was the middle of April, and Marsh's was one of the few things for tourists to do in Long Beach besides hanging out at the beach and taking bacon pictures.

Colette and my sister and I used to go to Marsh's with our piggy banks and buy saltwater taffy and have our fortunes told, then dare each other to look at Jake the Alligator Man for a full minute, which is super-tough because I'm telling you, that half-man, half-alligator thing looks completely gross. I still have some videos of us inside Marsh's saved somewhere. It was part of a game we used to play called dare-or-scare. It was cool.

Thinking of that made my tears dry up.

I wondered if Kai had gone to Marsh's after his interview at the police station; Kai's parents ran the store and they made him help sometimes even though I think that might be illegal. Part of me wanted to go apologize for being rude and part of me felt like he'd probably already gotten over it so what was the point.

"Hi, how are you feeling?" Mom asked carefully when she joined me near the frying pan.

"I'm okay," I said.

"Really?" I didn't like how surprised she looked, but I nodded anyway.

"Well, that's great," Mom said, "because they want you to come back in. Both you and Tess. I just got off the phone with her and she's on her way back. Another officer found something in Colette's locker that they want you to see."

"What?" I asked.

Mom shrugged; the sun blasted into my eyes when I looked up at her. "We'll find out soon," she said. "And I think they want to talk more about when you last saw Colette, too."

"Tess is a liar," I said matter-of-factly. I felt bad about saying it, but it had to be true because I knew I wasn't lying.

"Please don't call your sister names," Mom said, frowning.

Her long, dark brown hair blew up all around her like she was a superhero, and she should have just let it go, but she wrapped it into a lady-knot at the back of her head. Mom, Tess, and I all have the same hair color—except Mom's has some gray in it—but theirs is straight and usually clean and brushed, and mine is curly and usually dirty and wild. That's why I keep it shorter: brushing out snarls is the worst.

"I'm telling the truth," I said, pushing off the bench and walking back toward the police station. Mom followed me. "I know that Colette came to see me at six forty-five. I'm one hundred percent sure that's the right time."

"Frankie, I believe you. But do you think your sister would lie to the police?" Mom asked. "Do you honestly think that?"

"No one would ever think that Tess would lie to the police or do anything wrong," I said, trying to keep my tone of voice steady. "I am the person people would call a liar, no matter what." I blew my bangs out of my eyes; I needed a haircut, but I hated getting them. "I'm telling you the truth."

"I said I believe you," Mom said. "I believe that both of you *believe* you're telling the truth. But one of you must be wrong—by accident, of course."

"Let's just go in," I said. We were outside the police station again.

"We need to wait for Tess," Mom said, leaning to the left so she could see down the street, pulling her sweatshirt tight around her. "She'll be here soon."

"Fine."

———

IN THE SAME interview room as before, Officer Rollins dragged in another chair. Tess sat down in the one by the far wall, hunching forward like she always does, her arms wrapped tightly around herself.

"That's my seat," I said.

"It's not yours," she said quietly, pressing her lips into a line.

"It's the one I sat in before, so it's mine."

"I used this one when Mom and I came in earlier, too. Can't you just sit in the—"

"Tess," Mom said in a low voice.

"What?" Tess asked her quietly. "Can't she just sit in the other chair? This is mortifying."

"Can we get started?" Officer Rollins asked. "There are chairs for everyone."

"Yes, but she's in mine." I pointed at the new chair and said to Tess, "You can use that one."

"So can you?" Tess said like a question. She looked from me to Officer Rollins to Mom. Tess seemed really embarrassed and I didn't like it, but I couldn't stop myself from demanding that she give me the chair by the wall.

Sitting down in the chair that I was standing right next to would have been the easy thing to do. But sometimes I can't make myself do the easy thing.

"I can't sit near the door." My voice was sharper. I started to feel the tightness that happens in my throat before the tears show up. I could feel the scream building in me. Tess needed to *move*.

"You can have my chair," Mom said, getting up.

"You know I can't sit in the middle either." My arms were hanging by my sides, and I flipped my hands so that my palms were facing out, wondering if it'd work again. But it was hot in the room and my head itched and I had to scratch it, so I didn't keep my palms up for long enough.

"Ladies, we really need to get started," Officer Rollins said. He sounded annoyed.

"Tess, please," Mom said to my sister. She sounded desperate. Tears were rolling down my cheeks—I didn't notice them until one dripped into my mouth. I didn't like the warm, salty taste.

Tess stood up, scooted over, and dropped into the new chair with a *thud*, rewrapping her arms around herself and letting her hair fall over half of her face. She had tears in her eyes, too.

I wiped away my own and got into my chair as quickly as I could.

"Now that we're all settled," Officer Rollins said, "I'd like you to both see something we found in Colette's locker." He looked at Tess. "You share the locker with Colette?"

Tess nodded. "What is it?" she asked, sounding scared. It made me feel worse.

"It's a diary," Officer Rollins said.

I tilted my head to the side, picturing Colette taking

some diary with a unicorn on the cover to middle school. "What the heck?" I asked, sniffing because the tears had made my nose run.

"Frankie!" Mom said. "Manners, please."

"It's okay," Officer Rollins said to Mom. Then, looking at me, he said, "It's interesting that you ask that, Frankie, because your name is on it." I opened my eyes wide as he looked at my sister. "Yours too, Tess."

I leaned forward so I could see Tess around Mom. She did the same, the chair incident forgotten. Everyone in my family is used to my emotions.

"He's not talking about—" Tess started to say, but then stopped because she knew that I knew what she meant.

"No way," I said back to her. "It's in my room. In that place."

"I thought so, but then . . ." Her voice trailed off.

"Right?" I said. "How . . ."

"Exactly. And when . . ."

"I know, and . . ." I scrunched up my forehead. "I don't know."

We both looked back at Officer Rollins, who had a confused expression on his face. He cleared his throat. "Okay, then," he said. "I don't know if it's twin language or teen language, but either way, I'm definitely not fluent. Care to elaborate?"

"Huh?" I asked.

"Sorry," Tess said. She apologizes too much. "There's this notebook—"

"Could you speak up a little?" Officer Rollins asked. "I can barely hear you."

"Sorry," Tess said again, a bit louder. "There's this notebook we had when we were younger. Way younger, like in third grade. We wrote in it until the end of elementary school."

I talked over Tess. "None of us were ever in the same class in elementary school, so we wrote notes for each other and left them in a hiding spot in the library. We checked it when it was our class's turn to have library time."

"It was the way we stayed in touch." Tess looked down at her hands, then back at Officer Rollins. "It can't be what you're talking about, though, because Frankie has that notebook at home. And Colette wouldn't take it to school now."

"Did you?" Officer Rollins asked.

"No!" Tess said, her neck red and blotchy.

Officer Rollins bent over and picked up a big puffy envelope near his feet. It was the same envelope I'd seen the woman officer carrying a little while ago. Officer Rollins dumped its contents onto the table. All that was inside was a book inside a plastic baggie. A book that a grown-up might call a diary. The book that Tess, Colette, and I had called—

"Fred!" Tess shouted. "She had Fred!"

Seeing the notebook that Colette had asked me for the night before—the notebook that should have been in my room—was so confusing. I just stared at it for a few seconds, trying to work out how she could have gotten it. Unless it hadn't been in my room in the first place. But then, where had it been? Or unless she'd taken it from my room. But when? Besides eating dinner at the cottage, I hadn't left my room at all.

"Its name is Fred," Officer Rollins said, interrupting my thoughts. "I see."

The reason the diary's name was Fred was because I was a terrible speller when I was younger and I'd been trying to write *friend* on the cover, but I'd forgotten the *i* and the *n*. Thankfully, Tess didn't tell Officer Rollins that humiliating fact about me; instead, she just said, "We liked the name and it was part of our code. Like we'd pass each other in the hallways and whisper, 'Time to meet with Fred,' and none of the other kids would know what we meant."

"I see," Officer Rollins said, removing Fred from the table and putting it back inside the puffy envelope. "This has to go to forensics; I just needed to make sure that the notebook belonged to Colette."

"It belonged to me," I said.

Tess shook her head and said softly, "It belonged to all of us."

"Girls," our mom said sharply, warning us not to fight.

"Sorry," Tess said. I stayed quiet.

"It's okay," Officer Rollins said, smiling at Mom. "We made copies, so you can go through it at home and let us know if you see anything out of the ordinary." He cleared his throat. "It's a long shot, but we're researching every possibility."

"Can we leave?" I asked.

Mom gave me a look.

"In just a minute," Officer Rollins said. "I wanted to ask both of you again: What time did you see Colette last night?" He crossed his arms over his chest and waited.

"Six forty-five," I blurted out.

"What?" Tess asked defensively. "That's when she was in my room. Why would she be in yours?"

"Like she can't come to mine?" I asked back. "Like I have the plague or something?"

"That's not what I meant!" Tess said. "I meant that she ca—"

"Girls!" Mom said again, more serious this time. "Keep your tones down."

"Sorry, Mom," Tess said.

"Yeah, sorry," I mumbled.

I wasn't sorry, though. I was right.

———

Mom let Tess go off to help Mia make cookies for Colette's parents and flyers to hang up around town, but she made me walk home with her. It was another example of how she treats me like I'm a little kid even though Tess and I are the same age.

She started to ask me questions about the conversation with Officer Rollins, about Fred, about seeing Colette the night before.

"We're not talking about that stuff," I cut her off.

"Then tell me why you seem so angry at your sister lately."

She stole my only friend, I thought, but didn't say, because I wasn't sure if I completely believed it. If anyone had caused a change in our friendship status, it was Mia. But Tess *had* betrayed me, and I ended up friendless. So in a way Tess did steal my only friend—or friends, if you count a sister as a friend—or at least helped it happen. I wasn't about to say all of that to my mom, though: she'd just defend Tess.

"I don't know what you mean," I said instead.

We were walking down Pacific in the opposite direction of the inn. I'd chosen the path, and Mom hadn't said anything. She'd just started walking beside me, carrying my photocopy of Fred.

My hands itched.

"Okay . . . ," Mom said, "then why were you rude to Kai at the station. Did he do something to you?"

That was an easy one. "No," I said. "Kai is nice."

"I thought so," she said. "You two used to be such cute friends. Remember when you made up that language together at summer camp?"

I remembered getting laughed at by the other kids for making up my own language until Kai came over and asked if I would teach it to him, but I didn't say that. I didn't answer at all, and I think Mom understood that she was making me uncomfortable, so she got quiet and we walked in silence the rest of the way down Pacific.

My brain swirled and twisted. *Colette's gone. Why won't she just stop messing around and come back? I should be relaxing right now. Instead, I just left the police station! This is not how the day was supposed to go!*

My head itched. I walked next to my mom, past the kite shop with the blue horizontal siding and the gift shop with the barn-red vertical siding. I scratched my head and counted my steps from one antique streetlight to the next: twenty-two. From that light to the next, I took bigger steps: eighteen. I scratched my head again, noticing that we were almost where I wanted to turn left, so I stepped out between parallel-parked cars to cross. My arm was practically torn from my body when my mom grabbed it and yanked me backward.

"Ouch!" I shouted, pulling myself from her grip as a car horn blared. I flipped around and saw my mom, wide-eyed. "That hurt!" I yelled at her.

"You were almost hit by a car!" she yelled back.

"I saw it!" I shouted, rubbing my sore arm where she'd grabbed it. "I was going to stop."

"It didn't look like it," Mom said in a more normal voice. "Let's go to the crosswalk."

Between us, I hadn't seen the car. But that's not the type of thing you want to admit to your mom if you're trying to stay off medication and out of therapy.

Also, the speed limit is only twenty-five, which is around how fast tornadoes go, so I probably wouldn't have died. I read once that your chances of dying if you're hit by a car going that slowly are only three percent or something. I'm not sure I have that right, though.

Safely across the street, we turned left at Bolstad toward the ocean. Mom didn't say anything when we passed City Hall or the RV Resort; when we walked under the WORLD'S LONGEST BEACH sign and down the long row of beach parking spots.

"Can we take the boardwalk?" she asked. "I don't want to get sand in these shoes."

We were at the big red buoy in the center of the road, almost where the parking stops and the beach begins. You can either go forward out to the sand, turn left and walk the boardwalk, or turn back toward the town. Canada is to the right and Oregon is to the left, if you walk long enough.

I really like walking on the beach and normally would have suggested that my mom just take off her shoes if she didn't want sand in them, but I was so unsettled about all the change, I agreed. And I was glad almost immediately because the hollow *plunk* that the boards made with each of our steps was a beat that calmed me. Walking next to my mom calmed me, too.

"Are you worried about Colette, Frankie?" Mom asked in her soft voice. The wind whistled as it blew in the grass and I could see at least a dozen kites flying over the sand.

"Of course," I said quickly. "Who wouldn't be?"

"I wasn't asking about other people; I was asking about you," she said. "I know the last couple of months have been difficult for you . . ."

"You mean since I lost the only friend I've ever had?"

"I think people's perceptions of things are different," Mom said kindly. "Sometimes people remember things in a negative way while others may remember the experience differently."

"I guess," I said, watching the beach grass ripple like waves; I wished I could run through it and let it tickle my palms. "I don't know how anyone could see it differently, though. Colette made the choice not to be my friend."

"Huh," my mom said. "Is that how Colette would tell the story? That she chose not to be friends with you? Or would she say you got mad and told her you didn't want to hang out with her anymore?"

"By talking about me behind my back, she made the choice," I said. "It's her fault, not mine."

"Oh, Frankie, friendships aren't about fault," Mom said. "They're about forgiveness." She nudged my shoulder with hers; we were nearly the same height and had been since last summer. Tess was way taller. "And they're tough, especially when people grow up and change. You kind of have to keep getting to know your friends all the time. Want to know what other type of relationship is like that?"

"What?" I asked, not minding the conversation.

"Parent-kid relationships," she said. "You guys grow and change all the time and I have to keep trying to get to know the new you."

"I'm the same me," I said. "I haven't changed. Colette has." *Had?* "Mom?" I asked, looking up at her.

"Hmm?"

"What if Colette's dead?"

"Oh, my girl," Mom said, "I don't even want you to think that way. Colette's probably just fine."

Her tone didn't sound convincing.

"I *am* thinking that way, though," I said. "Mom, seriously, what if she's dead?"

Mom looked really sad. "I hope with all my heart that she isn't, for Colette's parents' sake, for Tess's and her other friends' . . . and for yours."

"Me too," I said, because no matter what, that much was true.

chapter 7

Fact: Three types of tornado alerts
are watch, warning, and emergency.

BACK AT HOME after the police station, I felt jumpy, like
during a tornado watch. That's when the weather conditions are right for tornadoes, but the weather people haven't
spotted any funnel clouds yet.

I kept looking out the window, like Colette was just
going to stroll up to the inn with a big smile on her freckled lips. Pacing, with Pirate watching me from the foot of
my bed without lifting her head, I asked Colette a string of
questions aloud.

"Where are you . . . and why was Fred in your locker?
How did you get Fred? And how the heck were you in my
room and Tess's at the same time? Why was Kai at the
police station? . . . Oh, and what's up with your weird boyfriend staring into space?"

Here's a tip about me: I have to have answers. If you tell me a riddle and I can't solve it fast, you just have to tell me the solution. And if you say you'll give me a present later, you might as well give it to me now, because otherwise I'll keep thinking about it like crazy until *later* comes. It's all I'll think about, not wanting to, like how you can't stop touching a hangnail or licking a mouth sore even when it hurts.

So yeah, I have to have answers. The world seems less overwhelming that way.

That's not the greatest way to be, though—at least not if you want to have a lot of friends. People don't always feel comfortable if you just ask them things. That's called "being direct" and most middle school kids I'd encountered so far didn't like it.

Except Kai.

I pulled out my phone and sent him a text. It'd been a long time since we'd texted. The last one I'd sent him was a whole six months earlier.

FRANKIE

Hi 👋 🏆 🍦

KAI

R U eating dessert in a tornado right now?!?

84

> LOL. No. Wondering why
> you were at the 🚕 ???

The dots did their dance for longer than I thought they should have, like Kai was really thinking about his answer. I was impatient.

> WELL?

she was at the store
last night
I was wkng

> ????

How should I know
Taking video selfies and stuff

> HUH
> Of what

Not talking . . .
Just standing there like a statue and freakin
out customers

> 🕐 ?

Around 8

That's what I told the cops

ur like them with the ???????

SNS

Sorry-not-sorry was basically my motto.

He sent a crying-laughing emoji with a wave.

One time, Gabe made me practice during one of our therapy sessions. That's an example of how my life is not normal—adults make me *practice* texting. Gabe told me how to look for signs that people were ready to stop a conversation and made me practice ending them. Because otherwise, I'd text people all night long. I mean, if I had anyone to text.

Bye Kai!

He sent another wave. I wanted to tell him that my previous text rhymed, but that would be continuing the conversation that Kai clearly wanted to end. So I put my phone on my nightstand.

It had been the longest, weirdest Friday ever. And still, dinner wouldn't be for a few hours. I needed something to take my mind off how strange the day had been, so I got the photocopied pages from the police station and started looking through them.

Fred, our notebook or diary or whatever you want to

call it, is about the size of a typical book, but the sheets of paper that Fred was copied onto were bigger, normal pieces of white printer paper. That meant that there was a fat margin between the edge of Fred and the edge of the copy paper—but whoever copied Fred had held him down flat through the process, so part of the person's arm was visible in the margin.

I got distracted and grossed out by the photocopied hairs from the copier's wrist appearing on every page. It took me a few minutes to get over that and start really reading.

When I did, I was embarrassed because stuff I'd thought was important as a third grader felt ridiculous now. The first few notes that Tess, Colette, and I left for each other in the library said things like:

Hi! How are you today?
Hi back! I'm fine how are you ☺
It's cold outside. I don't want to go to recess!
Mr. Ellensburg is so mean!
I wish my mom would let me have a guinea pig!

Most of the messages from Colette and Tess didn't really say much of anything. There were a lot of drawings of kids and tigers and rainbows and dolphins. My messages were more real. One from me to them said:

Emmy hit me in the face with the teltherbal at reces on purpos. Miss French didn't beleeve me that it was on purpos but Emmy laffed about it with her frends and they all made fun of me for crying. She sent me to the nurse since my face is all red. Emmy is mean!

The reply from Tess on the same page said:

She's mean! I'm sorry!

And under that, from Colette:

We beleive you Frankie I'm sorry your face hurts. I told Emmy I'm not going to her birthday party. She said she's having chocolate cupcakes and I said I didn't care because she was mean to my best freind. PS. Tess you're my best freind too.

After a half hour of reading the same type of messages, I decided that there was no way the stuff we'd written in third and fourth grade would help Officer Rollins with anything other than knowing which kids were mean in elementary and that Tess was already starting to be a decent artist.

I got some water from the mini-fridge in my room before continuing with Fred. I knew what was coming: the page about our dare-or-scare game. Chugging my water, I thought back to when we made up the game. It was during winter break in fifth grade and we were bored.

"I'm bored," I had complained to Colette and Tess.

"Me too," Colette complained back.

"Me three," Tess agreed.

We were on Colette's covered front porch, wearing loads of layers, squashed three across in an oversize porch rocker meant for two. It was overcast and too windy to go to the beach.

"We could climb the roof," Colette suggested. Her house is an A-frame; if you don't know what that looks like, imagine a normal two-story house with a triangular roof, then chop off its lower level so the sides of the triangle nearly touch the ground. It looks crazy, like a house that sank into the dirt.

"We did that yesterday," I said.

"I always slide back down," Tess said.

"That's because you don't climb the right way," I told my sister.

"Yes, she does," Colette said, sticking up for Tess. "It was slippery."

"We could do a quiz," I suggested, knowing I was right about climbing.

"Okay," Tess agreed.

"I'm over quizzes," Colette said, which hurt my feelings

a little since she knew I loved them. "Let's put on my mom's makeup!"

Tess's eyes widened, and she sat up straight, smiling. Maybe it was because she was artistic, but she was really good at putting on makeup. She looked at me to see what I thought of the idea.

"No way!" I blurted out. "I can't . . . ," I began, tripping on my words. "The brushes . . . my face . . . it's so . . ."

"It's okay, Frankie," Tess said, disappointed. "She doesn't like the feeling of the makeup on her skin," she told Colette.

"Oh," Colette said.

I felt like I'd let them down, that now I needed to come up with something really great. I considered what the three of us liked to do together. All I could think was that we could make up a game. But not just any game: the best game!

"Let's do truth-or-dare!" I said, jumping off the rocker because honestly I'd been too pinched in there for my liking. But I was on some medication that was keeping me from screaming about it, at least. Except it was the kind that made me feel shaky and hungry, so it still sucked.

I faced my friends. "We can make amazing dares!"

"I love that idea!" Tess said, beaming before her eyes clouded over. "Except we already know all of each other's truths." She bit her fingernail, thinking, then sat up straight with excitement. "How about dare-or-scare?"

Tess loves being scared or scaring people. You might think that's surprising since she's quiet and introverted and apologizes all the time and sometimes seems like she's afraid of the world. But it's a secret way Tess is really brave—braver than me.

"Um . . . ," I began, not into the "scare" idea.

"What do you mean?" Colette asked. She looked intrigued.

"Well, you can either do the dare," Tess said, "or you'll get a scare!" She laughed wickedly.

"I don't want to be scared," I said, flapping my hands. "You know I hate that."

"Then do all the dares." Colette laughed. She put her pointer finger to her mouth, thinking, then said, "Maybe one of the dares will be to hug a tombstone!"

"No!" I said, my eyes wide, my heart racing.

"That would be better than waiting for someone to jump out at you," Tess said. "And besides, you could do it in the daylight." I must have looked terrified, because Tess added, "We can choose a prize for the person who does the most dares."

"What kind of prize?" I asked.

"Taffy," Tess said confidently. Taffy from Marsh's was basically a food group.

"Good idea. Let's start making a list of dares," Colette said.

"Fine," I said, not liking the possibility of visiting the

graveyard but thinking that *I* was going to be the best at dares of all three of us. "I'm going to win and get all of your taffy."

"No, you're not," Tess and Colette said in unison, laughing.

Tess checked the time on the phone she'd gotten for Christmas. "Frankie and I have to be home at five," she said, frowning. "We need to do this fast."

"Hold on," Colette said, jumping up and running inside her house. She was back in seconds with Fred. "We can write the dares down in here."

To my dismay, the first thing Colette wrote was: Hug a tombstone. She nudged me and smiled, telling me I'd be okay. From there, we all shouted ideas, Colette scribbling down the ones that all three of us agreed on: Climb Colette's roof alone. Run your fastest from the inn to the water. Do jumping jacks in the middle of the arcade. And the list went on. We filled a whole page with dares, front and back. It took us so long to make the list that we didn't get to do any dares that day—or, thankfully, scares—but we started the game the next.

Now, in my room, a smile I hadn't even noticed building on my face melted away. Colette and I weren't friends anymore. Tess and I didn't have the same relationship either. They'd both betrayed me.

Sad, I picked up the photocopy of Fred and turned to

the next page, looking forward to going back in time and reading our list of dares. But the next page wasn't about dare-or-scare: it was another note about school. I flipped to the next, and it was doodles, mostly of tornadoes—by me, naturally. I turned all the rest of the pages that Officer Rollins had given me, completely confused. Either he hadn't given me a complete copy of the notebook, or someone had torn out one of the pages.

All I knew was that there was no mention of the dares or scares in my copy of Fred at all.

chapter 8

Myth: You can outrun a tornado.

"CHARLES, I'M BORED," I said, my chin resting on my hand, my elbow on the tall counter of the reception desk. *Bored* is my universal way of saying that I need something different to do, even if I'm not technically *bored*.

"Hmm," Charles said, his eyes on the Rubik's Cube in his hands. As he twisted the annoying puzzle over and around, I looked at the tattoos on his arms: the compass that was also a man's eye whose hair morphed into the ocean with an orca breaching. There wasn't any clear skin from his wrists to beyond his shirtsleeves. Way up on his shoulder, I knew he had a rose for his girlfriend before my mom, who died in a car accident. She's the reason Charles gave up his corporate-lawyer job and moved out to Long Beach, so she's the reason we know him at all, I guess. I was thinking about how much that probably hurt—the tattoos, I mean—when Charles said, "You could sweep the lobby."

"No way," I said.

"Bring in the cushions from the outdoor furniture? It smells like it's going to rain." The main door was propped open and when I took my next breath, I realized Charles was right.

"There are always bugs on the cushions," I said, shivering at the thought.

"Start a new pot of coffee?"

"You sound like Mom."

Charles looked up at me and smiled, the skin around his eyes crinkling. "Maybe she's right that I'm too soft on you and your sister."

"If I do the coffee, is it okay if I go for a bike ride?" I asked.

He looked from me to some guests getting out of their car in the lot; he'd have to check them in soon. He sighed and set aside his Rubik's Cube, then mussed up his own hair.

"I'm okay with fresh air in any capacity," he began, "but today's not a typical day, with Colette missing, and would you look at those clouds? It's going to pour."

"I like riding in the rain."

He scratched his head. "Did you ask your mom?"

"I can't find her," I said. It wasn't necessarily a lie, because I hadn't seen my mom on my way from my room down the hall and down the stairs to the lobby. But I hadn't looked for her either.

"I don't know, Frankie," Charles said, his eyes on the guests, who were loading up a luggage cart. "Do you have your phone with you?"

"Yes," I said, nodding.

"Okay, then you can ride for a half hour," he said, smiling at the guests as they came through the door. "Welcome," he said to them. He looked at me sternly, like a kid pretending to be a grown-up. "Be back in exactly thirty minutes."

"I will!" I called, not doing the coffee, waving behind me. With Charles engrossed in checking in the guests on the computer, I took one of the complimentary beach cruisers that people could use during their stay. He'd probably have said it was okay. Mom might not have. I had to take the green one because my favorite yellow one was still checked out.

I pedaled fast, picturing myself trying to outrun a tornado, looking back over my shoulder a few times on the way toward town, almost seeing it there behind me, just like the one in kindergarten. I imagined it crashing through the new fancy mini-golf course, sending golf balls flying;

bulldozing the theater, making popcorn swirl into the air; and tossing aside the hut where you sign up for horseback rides on the beach.

A horn beeped at me when I paused too long in the middle of an intersection, mesmerized by my imagination. It made me jump and forced me to focus on what was real, the imaginary tornado sucked back into the sky. I quickly rode on, coasting down a few blocks, past the lots of land for sale and two motels. On Bolstad, I turned left toward the ocean.

The dare-or-scare game on my mind, I passed the parking spaces and the buoy, then took another left on the paved bike path that would take me back in the direction of the inn. I was riding in a huge circle. Heavy gray clouds loomed overhead, but no rain fell yet. There was so much going on in my head that I could have ridden all the way to Oregon but there was no way to do that and get back in half an hour.

What I wanted to know was why the dare-or-scare page was missing from Fred. I felt like it meant something. And I didn't understand why or how Colette had had Fred in the first place: I felt like that meant something, too.

I pedaled fast and ducked quickly under the Decapitator, the part of the path that dips under the boardwalk. I passed the inn and kept on going. Houses were to my left, and grassy dunes with the ocean beyond them were to my right.

I didn't want to look left at a specific house for some reason. I didn't dwell on it.

Pedaling, pedaling, pedaling, my mind spun. I'd ridden this path so many times, I probably could have closed my eyes and still known when the curves were coming. I was free to think, think, think of dares.

Do a headstand.

Bark like a dog in the middle of the cafeteria.

Ding-dong-ditch someone's house.

Sing in public.

Stare at something gross for one minute.

Put on makeup without looking in the mirror.

Ask a total stranger for a french fry—and then eat it.

I felt like it was super-important to remember the dares we'd actually done. But no matter how hard I tried, I couldn't remember which we'd done, which had been rejected, and which I was coming up with right then and there. There were so many possible options: think of how many lines are on both sides of a piece of notebook paper!

"Ugh!" I shouted aloud. *I hate my stupid memory!* I shouted in my head, gripping the bike handlebars tight, wishing I knew why Colette had taken Fred, why the dare-or-scare page was missing, and why I was obsessed with remembering the challenges. Shouldn't I have been more concerned about where Colette was than about a stupid notebook and game? I knew I should've, and yet I couldn't stop myself from focusing on the wrong things.

Up ahead, there were two men sitting and smoking on one of the benches along the path. I didn't want to get near them or ride through their smoke cloud, so I stopped the bike hard, skidding, and turned around. I was sweaty and out of breath from pedaling so fast.

The wind was picking up and riding wasn't doing anything to organize my thoughts. I rode back without looking at one of the houses on the right. It made me feel uncomfortable. I didn't dwell on it.

Nearing home, I saw Tess and Mom walking toward the cottage: it must have been dinnertime. Instead of taking the cruiser to the lobby, I left it against the side of the building, then went to meet up with them. I was starving.

———

ON FRIDAYS, MY family makes pizza and plays board games together. Tonight, though, Charles was still working at the front desk, and Tess refused to play anything. She and Mia had taken their cookies to Colette's parents and Tess had been gloomy since she'd gotten back. I felt like there was something wrong with me because I still would have played a game despite maybe being worried about Colette. I don't really know what worry feels like.

We watched a movie instead, something about a girl and a horse. Tess picked it. Mom texted a lot during the movie and got up once to take a call from Colette's mom, which she took in her room with the door closed and which lasted for more than twenty minutes.

When she finally came back, her eyes looked red and puffy. "They still don't know anything," she said.

"Were you crying?" I asked.

"I'm okay," Mom said.

"That's not what I asked."

"I know," Mom said. "Should I make some popcorn?"

My mom's popcorn is the best on the planet, so I said yes and forgot about asking her about crying. We unpaused the movie, and it started raining sideways, the drops tapping on the window like fingertips on a clicky laptop keyboard. I burrowed under a blanket and, with my eyes on the screen, watching the girl with the horse grow up to overcome her challenges, I daydreamed about growing up and becoming a meteorologist or chasing tornadoes or texting through a boring movie or being liked for being nice and funny instead of disliked for being weird.

I daydreamed about Colette knocking on the door to my room and asking for Fred, and me saying yes instead of no. About me asking why she wanted it instead of ignoring her and putting on my headphones. I daydreamed about Colette apologizing about February and inviting me to go do a dare with her—and me agreeing. I daydreamed about winning her taffy but sharing it with her, too.

I daydreamed about Colette being not-missing.

And then I ran through a downpour to bed, and I night-dreamed about her being okay, too.

PART 2

A Bad Saturday

chapter 9

Fact: Tornadoes are born from thunderstorms.

"HEYA, FRANKIE."

"Hi, Teddy," I said to the high schooler behind the counter at the arcade. He was helping someone else, so I had to wait.

Even though my stomach hurt, I was at the arcade right when it opened at ten because going to the arcade was what I always did on Saturdays, and I needed to do what I always did instead of imagining Colette running away or being kidnapped or ripping out the dare-or-scare page from Fred and tearing it up to show me just how much we weren't friends anymore. Except, as mad as I was at her, I couldn't really picture Colette doing something like that.

It was a miracle my mom had let me come today with Colette missing and everything, but she'd been preoccupied by a guest who'd flooded his bathroom.

"Ready?" Teddy asked when it was my turn in line. I stepped forward, not looking at his face: his pimples made me cringe, but I concentrated on not commenting on them. Instead, I looked at the bulletin board on the wall behind Teddy. Colette's school picture stared back at me from a MISSING CHILD poster.

Teddy looked over his shoulder. "Oh hey, that's your friend, right?"

"No," I said. "Can I get my card?"

"What's the password?" he asked.

I rolled my eyes. "The password is 'Give me my card.'" A pain stabbed my lower belly and I wondered if something I'd eaten was making me sick.

"Geez," Teddy said, opening the register and retrieving my preloaded game card. Once a month, my mom put money on it and when it was out, it was out. I left it here so I wouldn't lose it in my bedroom or on the way home or at school or anywhere else I went. Keeping track of things isn't my superpower. "Here you go," he said, handing it over. "Some kid puked by the new shooter, so I'd steer clear of that corner."

"Thanks for the tip," I said, taking the card and turning toward the side of the sprawling space farthest from barf corner.

There were a lot of people there already because Saturday was two-for-one day and people in Long Beach like a deal.

I walked through bodies in the direction of my favorite starting point, Skee-Ball, with my chin awkwardly raised. I have to keep my chin up so that I can't see the carpet in my lower field of vision. It's black with blue swirls and red and yellow psychedelic stars intertwined among the swirls. It's dizzying and is, hands down, the worst thing about the arcade. The flashing lights and noises never bother me, because they're both expected—that's what arcades look and sound like—and because they are constant. But I really hate the carpet.

It's tough walking with your chin up at the arcade because the floor isn't level and twice—near the grabby-claw games and over by the big screens where you slash fruit—the floor either dips or rises, depending on where you're coming from.

Today, I stumbled a little by the grabby claw but made it to the Skee-Ball station without falling. But then someone was on the left-most Skee-Ball game, which is the only one I play, so I had to wait. I felt like there was a thunderstorm brewing inside me I was so impatient.

The player was a little girl who only got the ball into the lowest ring every time, so she should have been done quickly. I stood uncomfortably close to her side—this is what kids do to tell the world *I'm next*, so I had to do it even though it made my thighs feel weak. I whispered for her to hurry up under my breath, and to speed things along,

I picked up the ball for her when she threw it so hard it bounced off the side and onto the dreaded carpet.

I've played Skee-Ball a lot, so I knew when she was almost done with her game. And right then, some other kid—maybe her older brother—and some adult—probably their dad—walked up. When the girl finished her game, the dad swiped the other kid's card and let him go.

"Hey!" I said loudly, the storm inside me building. "It was my turn!"

The dad looked at me, surprised. "Oh, I'm sorry, I didn't see you there. We'll be done in just a few minutes."

I grumbled out loud.

The man looked at me. "The other two lanes are open. You could use one of those?"

"I like this one," I informed him, folding my arms over my chest. "I'll wait."

I screamed at them in my head, trying to ignore the pain in my stomach, until they finally left.

I stepped up to my Skee-Ball lane. Still annoyed about having to wait, I missed the first one, but then every ball I threw went in the tiny top circle. It was my highest score ever.

I went and checked the balance on my card and decided that I could play five more games, so I'd still have enough money on the card next weekend and the following. Thinking of next weekend made me think of Colette, and

I wondered whether she'd be safe back at home by then or whether . . .

I shook my head and went to the riding-motorcycle-race game. There was only one, and thankfully it wasn't taken, so I hopped on and chose the setting where you race through a field. I have to admit that I always picture a tornado bouncing along beside me as I'm racing. One thing on my list of things to do in life is to write the game company that makes it and tell them that the field level would be way better with the addition of a tornado.

I placed third, which was not good enough. I reached forward and slid my card through the reader again. But the screen continued to flash INSERT COINS. I tried the card reader three more times and it didn't work. I knew I'd have to go tell Teddy, but I didn't want to get off the motorcycle because it's a popular game and I just knew some little kid was going to come steal it. Maybe even the Skee-Ball lane thieves. I sat there debating my options for a while, wondering if maybe Teddy would just walk by. He didn't, though. Finally I got up.

"The card reader's broken on the motorcycle game," I told Teddy, facing away from the counter, my eyes on the bright yellow motorcycle. "Can you fix it?"

"I'll have to call the manager," Teddy said. "Card readers are his area."

"But I have to play it!" I protested. "I got third and I need to do better, or I'll be thinking about that the rest of the day!"

"I feel ya," he said. I heard him open the register again. "Here, use these tokens. They'll work."

I turned around and smiled at Teddy. "Thank you!" I said enthusiastically. He looked surprised, like he'd never heard me say that before.

I took the coins and rushed back to the yellow motorcycle, my chin up high to avoid carpet-spotting. Three kids from my school were approaching from the other direction. I grabbed the right handlebar of the motorcycle at the same time that a girl from my science class grabbed the left. Her blond hair was in a high ponytail with a huge polka-dot bow on top that looked really weird.

"I was here first," I said quickly.

"You were not," the girl said, looking me up and down. "Where's Tess?"

I sighed heavily. I'd heard that question about one million times in my life. "Who knows?"

"Really?" the girl asked, her eyes wide, her hand still on the handlebar. "That's surprising. I mean, doesn't she have to like babysit you when you come here?"

"No!" I said loudly. "She doesn't *babysit* me. We're the same age! We're twins!"

"Yeah, but you don't look anything alike," the girl's friend said, frowning at my outfit. She had a huge hair bow, too.

"Duh, we're *fraternal* twins." I tightened my grip on the motorcycle handlebar.

"You just seem . . . younger," the girl from my science class said, smiling in a mean way, making her friends giggle behind her.

"Whatever," I said, but it didn't feel like whatever. My stomach ached and there was a lump growing in my throat. "Just move over, I'm going to play this game."

The girl shrugged, her gaze falling to the seat of the motorcycle as she was turning to leave. "Ew, gross," she said. Her friends leaned in to look and they all grossed out in unison. "Have fun with that!" the girl called over her shoulder at me. Laughing, they walked away.

I looked down at the seat of the motorcycle, rolling the tokens Teddy had given me around in my hand. There was a reddish-brown streak across the seat. I stared at it for a few seconds, my eyebrows furrowed. I wondered if someone else had gotten on the seat without me seeing, but they couldn't have: I'd been watching the whole time. Then I wondered if it'd been there when I'd played the first time . . . and if I had something on my pants. *Gross!*

With my free hand, I brushed the back of my jeans to see if anything felt off. Sure enough, I felt wetness. I looked at my hand, and my fingertips had a faint red tint to them. Immediately, I was angry that someone had spilled something on the seat and left it there for the next person. *I can't believe what some people—*

And then I got it.

There I was, standing in the middle of the arcade, with tons of people there for two-for-one Saturday around me, and *THIS*. As if to say *duh!* the pain in my stomach I'd been experiencing dug in like when a cat doesn't want to be picked up.

I felt the color drain out of my face and turned so my back was to the machine. I looked down at my medium-blue jeans and pulled my sweatshirt down as far as it would go, which was only to my hips.

There aren't bathrooms in the arcade. You can use the outdoor public bathroom or go to one in a restaurant.

What do I do? I thought to myself. *Help! What do I do? Ohmygod, what do I do?*

Tears came to my eyes and my heart sped up. I'd read about all this stuff, and had sat through health class at school, but for some reason, I'd thought it wasn't going to happen to me. I especially hadn't expected it *today*. I dug my nails into my fists, the right fist wrapped around the tokens so tightly they were poking into my skin, too. My breaths were short and fast. A kid at a game next to me looked over, got scared, and ran off. The carpet was swirling. I felt dizzy and hot and helpless, my eyes moving back and forth over the room, searching for anywhere—anywhere!—to hide and think. *Tess would definitely know how to handle this problem without having a breakdown,* I thought. Panicked, I kept looking for a place to go. That's when I saw the door to the laser tag room. Without thinking about it, I darted across the arcade and slipped inside.

The overhead lights were off, but the fluorescent lights were on: bright green and pink and yellow beams told players how to get through the arena. I could hear players up ahead as I made my way down the dark path. I slipped between the partitions and felt my way to a corner that wasn't meant to be part of the game. I slid to the floor and got out my phone.

A memory popped into my head. In fourth grade, a group of girls in my class had coated a soccer ball in mud and thrown it at me at recess because I'd told one of them she looked like my grandma in her new glasses—which had been a fact and which had not been a bad thing, in my opinion. The girl had not agreed. When Colette saw the huge brown stain covering my new shirt and the huge tears in my eyes from being hurt on the outside by the ball and on the inside by the girls, she gave me her sweater. It was a freezing day, but she gave it to me anyway. If we were still friends, if Colette wasn't missing, she'd help.

Slumped in the corner of the laser tag arena, I wiped away tears, debating who to text. It was either Mom or . . . Tess.

FRANKIE

Tess!

I need ur help RIGHT NOW

COME 2 THE ARCADE

She didn't understand what I meant at first.

TESS

Frankie, come on

I don't want to play games

I'm not playing games

I got my YOU KNOW WHAT

What are u talking about?

ARE U SERIOUS

I GOT THAT THING!

u know what I mean right

She'd gotten hers last winter, and I couldn't believe she didn't understand what I was talking about.

Frankie, will u just say what u mean?

I'm worried about Colette

I seriously don't want to go
to the arcade today . . .

maybe next week

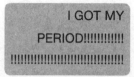

I GOT MY
PERIOD!!!!!!!!!!!!!
!!!!!!!!!!!!!!!!!!!!!!!!!!!!!!!!!!!!!

She didn't respond for a few seconds, which felt more like an hour.

Omg Frankie!

So awesome!

I did *not* think it was awesome in the slightest bit, and I couldn't figure out why Tess or anyone else would think it was. It felt squishy and wet and dirty and crampy and I wanted to teleport myself home and take a shower. And that was saying a lot because I hardly ever wanted to take showers. I didn't say all that to Tess because I just wanted her to stop texting me and get here already.

Hurry up!!!

I will!

Are you ok?

Yes of course

it's not like I'm dying

Just can't walk out of here

I'm in the laser tag area

HURRY UP

Do u have a sweatshirt to tie around ur waist or something?

I rolled my eyes, because of course I already thought of that, but I hate wearing too many layers, so all I had on under my sweatshirt was a bra.

Walking out of here in a bra is worse than with grossness on my jeans

Whaaaaaa?

Never mind hurry up!!!

Tess did come through for me, getting to the arcade in less time than I thought it would take. She brought a dark sweatshirt that entirely covered my stained jeans and walked her bike alongside mine back to the inn. Plus, she offered to help me when we made it to our rooms. There was no way I was letting anyone get near the bathroom door, and I could read a tampon box perfectly well on my own, but it was nice that she'd offered.

For a second, I forgot that she'd betrayed me a few months ago.

For a second, I had my sister.

chapter 10

Fact: For around twenty-five percent of
tornadoes, you get no emergency warning at all.

"IS EVERYTHING . . . OKAY?" Tess asked quietly, glancing down at my replacement outfit: jeans with holes and a gray hoodie, wet at the top from my dripping hair. Tess was in the doorway of her room; I was out in the hallway. "I mean, are you feeling okay?"

"I'm fine," I said, not getting why everyone had to make such a big deal about everything. I like to just handle things and move on. "Here's your sweatshirt." I held it out to her.

"Thanks," she said, walking over and dropping it in the hamper.

"It's not dirty," I said defensively. I'd only had it around my waist for fifteen minutes.

"I wore it riding yesterday," she explained. "It needs to

be washed." She looked at me for a second. "You don't have to stand in the door, you know. You can come in."

I hadn't been in her room recently. It felt strange to step inside.

Tess's room looks exactly like mine—except totally different. We have the same furniture and layout, but her comforter has bright flowers and mine is solid gray. Her walls are covered with inspirational posters and her own drawings of landscapes and people and abstract shapes; mine have pictures of tornadoes from the internet, a map of where the most serious ones have happened, and some sticky notes about things I want to remember. Like passwords and stuff. Her bed is made and, unless someone else snuck in and did it for me, which I hate, mine is not. Her books are on the shelf. Her pencils are sorted by shade in a see-through case. Her clothes are in the closet. Mine... aren't.

Tess sat down on the chair by her desk, her left leg folded so she was sitting on her foot. It reminded me of where I'd been sitting in my own room when Colette had been the one near the door two nights ago. Have you ever been to a rodeo when they open the bullpen and the bull charges out? That's what it felt like, only the bull was all the questions I had about Colette and Fred and dare-or-scare bucking around in my brain again.

"Did you notice that the page about dare-or-scare was

missing from the copied pages of Fred?" I asked my sister. "The one with all the dares listed out?"

"Not really," she said, biting her thumbnail.

If Mom were here, she'd tell Tess to stop. Here's a weird thing about us: Tess eats off her nails so there are no white parts showing at all. She always has. I think she does it when she's stressed or maybe she just thinks fingernails are gross. But I don't like having my nails clipped because it feels totally disgusting to me, so my nails are really long. See? Opposites.

"Do you think the police tore it out?" I asked.

Tess looked at me funny. "No, I don't think they'd do that."

"Well, do you think Colette did?"

"I don't know, Frankie, why would she?" Tess seemed to realize she'd been biting her nails and stuck her hands under her thighs.

"Maybe she thought it was embarrassing. Or maybe she ripped it up to be mean to me. Or maybe—"

"What are you talking about?" Tess interrupted. "Colette would never do something *mean* to you on purpose."

"Uh-huh."

"She wouldn't!" Tess said. "Colette has always lov—"

"I want to remember the dares we had listed in Fred," I interrupted loudly. I didn't want to talk about how Colette really would do something mean to me—and had. "Tess, it's *important*."

"Why?" Tess asked, chewing her nail again. "You don't think that the dare-or-scare challenge has anything to do with Colette being missing, do you? Because those were just silly dares, like jumping off the dune and landing without falling. They're not—"

"I just want to remember them," I said quietly. "I don't like when I can't remember things." Or maybe it was something more—something nagging at me that I didn't want to tell Tess.

"There were a lot," Tess said, getting up and starting to put away the folded laundry from the pile at the end of her bed. "I don't remember all of them either. It's not just you." I didn't answer, so she added, "Just look at that old Viewer account where we stored the videos."

I smacked myself on the forehead because I hadn't thought of that. Sometimes you can't see the easy answer, even if it's right in front of you. Pulling out my phone, I sank down to the floor and sat, cross-legged, eyes on the screen.

"You can sit in a chair," Tess said.

"Uh-huh," I murmured, not moving as I typed in the address for Viewer, and the password that only Colette, Tess, and I knew. "I haven't been on this account in so long," I said, clicking to open a video. "This is weird."

Tess sat down on the floor next to me and leaned in; I tilted the phone so she could see. She smelled like fruity shampoo. Tess might have been the only person who could sit that close to me without it bugging me—particularly at this point in time, with no medication, limited therapy, and a missing . . . person.

"Look," I said, my voice fading away as we watched a video of sneakers zipping through beach grass past a phone that'd been propped on something. "It doesn't have sound," I observed.

"I don't remember that dare," Tess said quietly. Then, after a few seconds, she asked, "Didn't we make all of the videos together? Why isn't someone holding the camera? Why is it propped up?"

"I don't know," I said to her too-many questions, "but those are Colette's shoes." I'd never owned a pair of vintage white sneakers because the rubber tops make my toes claustrophobic, and Tess's feet are too wide for that brand.

"No, they're not," Tess disagreed.

"Yes, they are," I said. "I'll play it again, look." I started the video over, pausing it when the feet were the closest. "Definitely Colette," I said. "She had on those sneakers Thursday night."

Tess flinched at the mention of the last night we saw Colette. I didn't say anything about the fact that we both thought that Colette had come to our rooms at the same time—and neither did she.

"But this was made two *years* ago, Frankie," Tess said, pointing at the post's date. "It must have been one of the last ones we made. We were probably eleven? Anyway, Colette's taller than her mom now and her feet are huge. She wasn't wearing the same shoes Thursday night as she wore in fifth grade when we did dare-or-scare. They wouldn't fit."

I shrugged, pretty sure that the dirty white sneakers on-screen were the ones I'd stared at when I hadn't wanted to look Colette in the eye two nights before—but sometimes I'm wrong about things. The video *did* say it'd been posted two years ago. Maybe she'd bought a bigger pair of the shoes she'd had in fifth grade.

Or maybe . . .

Something felt off. My stomach hurt—and it wasn't cramps this time. I didn't remember filming the video, but it reminded me of others we'd made. But there were so many that they were all jumbled up in my brain.

I went to another video, the next one in line. This time, the camera climbed someone's porch with whoever was holding it. The person reached out to set down a bunch of flowers in front of the door and I got a glimpse of a dark windbreaker. The person rang the doorbell then turned and ran back down the steps, the camera bouncing and making me feel sick. Then the screen went dark.

"Whose house is that?" I asked.

"Do you remember that one?" Tess asked back. "It looks like the ding-dong-ditch dare?"

I told her I did, but not with flowers, and I couldn't

recognize the house from just the steps, and I started the video again, immediately getting sucked in by the weirdness of it. This one didn't have sound either.

"Frankie! Stop ignoring me. Do you remember this video?" Tess asked, sounding annoyed.

"I answered you."

"No, you didn't!"

Didn't I? I wondered at myself. Sometimes I think I've said things because I hear them so loudly in my head, in my own voice. But I forget to actually say them out of my mouth. Except then I think I did, and that gets confusing for people. And for me.

"No, I don't remember it," I said . . . out loud . . . for sure.

I clicked on the next video. This one was, without a doubt, Colette. It was a video of her profile, her hair pulled back in a knot, wearing a white T-shirt. She was just standing there, not moving, for a full minute. She was inside somewhere, and the video was grainy, like the person holding it hadn't quite focused on Colette's face when they'd started recording. But then I noticed something.

"She's in Marsh's," I said. "See?" I pointed at the blurry shape behind Colette: one of the stuffed dead animals that hang from the ceiling of the store.

"Maybe," Tess said, leaning in closer. "I guess it's possible, but—"

Her phone chimed loudly; it made me jump. I hate phone sounds, so I always keep my phone on silent. Tess leaned away from me so she could get it out of her pocket. The warmth that'd been trapped between our touching arms and legs was released. I shivered.

I stared at the video and wondered if it was the selfie video Kai had told me about yesterday when we'd texted. The one that Colette had taken Thursday night. Except I didn't think that Colette was wearing the same T-shirt in the video that she'd worn to my room. In my room, she'd had on . . . I didn't remember.

Oh, dolphins.

There were only four videos on our account. There should have been way more. Had someone deleted the others? Everything felt off.

"Tess, I really think that Colette might have been doing our dares again."

"It's Mia," Tess said, ignoring me, eyes on her phone. "She's upset because someone drew on one of her flyers. She wants to come over."

"Fine," I said, standing up abruptly, blazing mad. Sometimes I wish my anger would have an emergency system, but it doesn't. Like a tornado showing up without any warning at all, I went from calm to completely annoyed that Tess wasn't listening to me because my gut told me that we should be paying attention to these old videos and she clearly didn't have the same feeling. No one ever listened to what I had to say. "Whatever."

"What's wrong?" Tess asked without looking up from her phone, her dark hair covering half her face, her thumbs flying over the keys.

"Nothing," I said. "I'm leaving."

"Okay, bye," Tess said softly, which sucked. I slammed the door to her room, wishing she had told me to stick around. Wishing she'd have a gut feeling, too; that she'd get obsessed with the missing dare-or-scare page and the videos with me. There were only four videos instead of what should have been about a million. Or at least twenty. I needed to know where the others were—and I wished Tess needed to know, too.

But, as usual, she had better things to do.

chapter 11

Fact: Even though it feels like longer, the average
tornado is on the ground for less than ten minutes.

"Is Officer Rollins here?" I asked the lady at the front
desk of the police station. I leaned my elbow on the high
counter and squashed my cheek against my fist. "I have
something to tell him."

It was twelve thirty on Saturday. After I'd left Tess's
room, I'd eaten lunch at the cottage with my mom—but
I'd pretty much run away after inhaling a sandwich so I
wouldn't have to hear more questions about my first period.
Didn't she remember her own?

"I'm sorry, Officer Rollins is out, honey," the front desk
lady said, her eyes on something behind me.

I turned around to see what she was looking at. As far
as I could tell, it was nothing. I hate when people do that.
"Made you look" is the worst game ever.

"I can call him for you, if you like?" the lady asked. I didn't answer, so she went ahead and dialed on a black phone on her desk. She talked for a few seconds, then held out the receiver. "Here you go, honey."

I took it and put it to my face, feeling awkward being tethered by a cord to a phone that was tethered to the wall, wondering how many germs might be transferring themselves from the receiver to my cheek right now.

"Hello, Frankie," Officer Rollins said. "Mary says you have something to tell me?"

I felt self-conscious. "Yeah . . . uh . . . so there's a page missing from that notebook you copied for me and Tess, did you notice that?"

"Sorry, Frankie, I can't hear you," Officer Rollins said. There were other voices in the background. "Will you please speak up a little?"

I tried again at volume three. That's more like the volume you need for presenting a report in class, but it was loud wherever Officer Rollins was. Except it sounded like I was yelling in the quiet police station. "The notebook you copied has a page missing from it—unless you didn't give me all of them."

"We gave you all of them," Officer Rollins said. "What was on the missing page?"

"It's a list of dares," I said. "It was part of this game we made up in fifth grade called dare-or-scare."

"I see," Officer Rollins said. "And?"

"And we made videos of us playing the game and put them on a Viewer account and I watched them—well, not those that we made but other ones, maybe newer ones?—because I think Colette was wearing the same shoes in videos that she had on when she came over Thursday night. I mean, I'm not positive, but I think so. They look the same."

The front desk lady was typing something but glancing at me every so often. I turned so my back was to her.

"I see," Officer Rollins said again, his voice sounding like he didn't see.

I thought maybe I hadn't said it right. "The videos say they were added to the account two years ago, but I think they were the same shoes she had on when I saw her, so maybe you could investigate or whatever . . ."

I paused, wondering what I'd hoped he could do with the videos. Now this trip seemed silly and I wondered if Tess had been right not to get obsessed with the videos like I had.

Officer Rollins was quiet, so my brain wandered off like it does sometimes.

I wonder if he's quiet because he's reading my mind, I thought. *That would be a cool superpower. What would I choose as my top five superhero powers? Flying, teleportation—*

"What shoes was she wearing in the videos?" Officer Rollins interrupted my list.

"White sneakers," I said confidently.

"Hmm," Officer Rollins said. I could hear pages turning. "Her parents told us she left the house in flip-flops Thursday night." He paused. "You said the videos are two years old?"

"Well, I mean, that's what the *account* says," I said, "but I think it's wrong."

"But that's what the account says," he repeated.

My face felt hot and I knew it was red; the more people told me I was wrong, the more positive I was that Colette had been wearing white sneakers the night she'd come to ask for Fred and that she'd been wearing the exact same shoes in the videos on Viewer. And that the videos were new and not two years old!

"Maybe her parents remembered wrong," I said.

"Maybe," Officer Rollins said. "People can do that in stressful times like this." Then he added slowly, "They can also make connections that may not be there." I wondered what he meant by that as he kept talking. "Thank you for calling, Frankie. Every tip helps, and I've written down this information and will keep it in mind. Please call me if you think of anything else."

"Okay," I said quietly, feeling like I'd screwed something up, but not knowing what. "Bye."

I handed the receiver back to Mary, the front desk lady,

and turned to leave. I watched my shoes as I walked across the lobby toward the door, spinning about Colette's sneakers, knowing I was right—just knowing it. *Tess doesn't think so*, I thought, *and neither does Officer Rollins. But does Kai? He saw Colette that night, too. I have to go find him and as—*

I slammed right into a wall.

"Ouch!" I shouted, my eyes stinging and watering; I'd hit my nose. Covering my face, I looked up and realized I hadn't hit a wall. Instead, I'd hit a person: the very worst person in town. She's the grouchy old lady who yells at everyone, both people who live in Long Beach and the tourists.

I had run into the Sea Witch.

"Pest!" she snapped in her Russian or Polish or whatever accent, glaring down at me with her glassy gray eyes.

She may have been old, but with a square jaw, shoulders almost as wide as a man's, and a biting tone, she was terrifying. I probably would have yelled at anyone else to *watch out!* but not the Sea Witch.

Stepping away from her, I muttered, "Excuse me," as quietly as Tess talks sometimes, so quietly I don't know if the Sea Witch heard me. We were in the doorway to the police station: her in and me out. My bike was leaning against a planter only a few feet away. I plotted making a run for it.

That's when she grabbed my wrist with her bony fingers. My heart felt like it would jump out of my chest because being touched by her was both scary and terrible at the same time. "You children with no supervision! Running around like you own this place!"

"Let go of me!" I shouted. Mary stood up from her desk and hurried toward us.

The Sea Witch leaned so close to my face that I could smell her sour breath. In a low voice, she said, "You never know what may happen to bad children running around with no parents." She let go of my wrist. "Be careful, you."

I ran to my bike, my heart pounding, breathing hard. It felt like I'd been through something terrifying, like a tornado had ripped through the police station. It was hard to calm down. Checking my phone, I realized I'd only been at the station for ten minutes. When bad things happen, I guess ten minutes can feel like much longer.

———

"FRANKIE, ARE YOU okay?" Kai asked from behind the smaller checkout counter at Marsh's. He had on a navy-blue T-shirt and a yellow beanie pushed back on his head, his wild hair sticking out in front. He was looking at me funny. "You look crazy-pale."

"Oh," I said, sinking my hands into a bin of polished sea glass to try to calm my racing heart. Walking my bike slowly across the street from the police station hadn't helped. I was sweating, too. It was always so hot in Marsh's. "Yeah,

I just . . . Never mind." I didn't want to relive it. I reminded myself why I'd wanted to find Kai in the first place: the videos. "Can we go outside for a minute?"

"Sure," Kai said, nodding. "Gotta tell my mom first. I'll meet you out there."

The fresh air was the best after being inside stuffy Marsh's. I sat on a bench facing the parking lot and the street beyond, my eyes watching the police station like a hawk. *What are you doing there?* I wondered at the Sea Witch. *Did you do something wrong?* I shook my head at myself, thinking that people didn't just walk into the police station if they were the ones who had done something wrong—they were escorted. At least on TV. *But then what were you—*

"I have five minutes," Kai said, making me jump. "Geez, Frankie, is everything all right?"

"I'm fine," I snapped before taking a deep breath and pulling my phone from my pocket. "Anyway, the reason I'm here is . . ." I turned toward him, quickly scrolling to Viewer on my phone. I shoved it in his direction. "Is this the video Colette made when she was here Thursday night?"

Kai took the phone and his eyes widened. "Frankenstein!" I frowned at Kai's latest nickname for me but let him talk. "I totally think it is! Where'd you get this?"

"That's not important." I brushed off his question. "The important thing is that you think it's the video she took."

"Yeah, her hair was pulled back like that."

"Did you notice her shoes?" I asked, hopeful. He shook his head.

"Naw, but that's right where she was standing when she came in," he said, pointing to a black curtain in the background of the video. "She's behind the fortune-teller." He paused, then added, "It's weird, but I think she might have stolen my jacket."

"What?" I asked, looking at him funny.

"Nothing."

I didn't care about Kai's jacket. I thought he'd probably left it at the boardwalk or something. "You're sure about where she was standing?"

"I think so?" Kai said, shrugging.

"No one believes me about Colette making that video on Thursday night," I said.

"Huh," Kai said. "Sorry." He waited a second and then said, "It was weird. Like I said, I wasn't really paying attention because my mom was making me haul boxes around in back when Colette was here. I need to join a club or something so she'll stop making me help out all the time."

As he went on, the Sea Witch popped back into my head. I was bugged by how she'd grabbed my wrist. How she'd told me to be careful. *Be careful of what?*

I forced myself to refocus on the video. It wasn't well-lit or flattering, and it didn't have anything interesting in it. Just Colette. Staring.

Kai's mom popped her head out and told him to please hurry up, the register lines were getting long, then disappeared again.

Kai stood, shoving his hands in his pockets. "I guess it's been five minutes already."

"Hey, will you show me where Colette was standing?"

He looked over his shoulder at the door.

"Really quick?" I pleaded.

"Okay," he said. "Come on."

Kai turned, and I followed him back inside, a double *ding-ding* sounding as we walked through the door. We snaked past the taffy and the ornate collectible dragons, the aisles of plastic toys for kids, and the racks of T-shirts and sweatshirts in every color of the rainbow. On the wood-paneled walls there were heads of dead animals, feathers from dead animals, and framed pictures—of dead animals. They were all for sale, but I didn't know why anyone would ever want to buy them. Marsh's is the weirdest "museum" I've ever seen.

I smeared sweat into my bangs, probably making them look really bad, but I didn't care. I was so focused on stuffed dead animals that I almost ran into Kai when he stopped abruptly. There was a stuffed spider monkey overhead and it looked like it was laughing at me.

"See?" he said, pointing at the back of the fortune-teller machine. He glanced at my bangs but didn't say anything.

"Colette took a selfie video while looking at these tiny license plates with people's names on them?" I asked, more confused than ever. "Why's it always so *hot* in here?"

Kai wasn't sweating despite his beanie. He answered my first question, but not my second.

"Oh, wait. No, she was facing this way," he said, turning around. I copied him, turning around kind of slowly, trying to imagine Colette standing right here.

Then I saw what she'd been looking at and gasped. Kai looked at me, confused. I didn't explain, though; my wheels were spinning faster than anything I could put into words. In five seconds, I'd be back on the beach cruiser, racing toward the inn. All that I said to Kai before bolting out of the store was:

"I know how to find Colette."

———

I KNOCKED ON Tess's bedroom door and when she opened it, I remembered Mia was coming over . . . since Mia was curled up like a cat on Tess's bed, her curly blond hair tied up in a topknot. She had mascara under her eyes like she'd been crying. My eyes got stuck on that for a few seconds; she wears too much makeup. *How much time do you spend doing that every morning? Why would you put on makeup today, if you're so upset that you're just going to cry it off?*

"Hi?" Tess asked, pulling my attention back to her.

"I need to talk to you," I whispered.

"Sorry, I'm kind of busy," she said in a low tone, gesturing at Mia, who was always dramatic. I don't get why Tess and Colette are friends with Mia. I mean, I guess she is student body president, and always coming up with ways to help students, like campaigning for gender-neutral bathrooms and better lunch options. And she volunteers to spend time with old people. But in my opinion, Mia does things to seem nice when really, she's not.

"Just come to my room for two minutes," I said bossily. "It's important."

Tess sighed and told Mia she'd be back in a second, which made Mia sigh. I've noticed that teen girls do a lot of sighing. Cats and dogs also sigh. Pirate is the queen of the dog sighers.

"What's going on?" Tess asked, following me next door to my room, which was unlocked because it always is, which my mom doesn't know. The curtains were billowing in because of a building late-afternoon storm. I turned and faced Tess; she was frowning at the mess all over my floor.

I thought of telling her about running into the Sea Witch, but for some reason, I didn't. Instead . . .

"Colette made the videos Thursday night and she was doing dare-or-scare for sure!" I blurted, the syllables bumping into one another as they fell out of my mouth.

"What?" Tess asked like she hadn't been listening. I

repeated myself—faster and louder and bumpier. Afterward, she asked, "Why do you think that?"

"I went to Marsh's and Kai showed me where Colette stood when she went there Thursday night when she was taking selfies—except she wasn't taking selfies! She was looking at Jake the Alligator Man and taking a video of herself doing it! It's the dare where you had to look at something gross!"

"Wait," Tess said, confused, "you didn't tell me that Colette was in Marsh's."

"Yes, I did," I said, confidently unsure. "Why do you think Kai was at the police station?"

"I don't know, but no, you didn't tell me," Tess said, confidently confident.

"Yes, I did," I insisted. Then quickly I added, so she couldn't get the airspace to disagree again, "The point is that she made a video of herself staring at Jake!"

Tess looked like she was thinking, then said, "That does seem like the dare we made . . ."

"I know!" I said. "That's what I'm telling you!"

She tucked her dark hair behind her ear and started biting her pointer fingernail, her eyebrows pulled together. Her eyes are like a mood ring, and today, they matched the overcast sky. "That's really weird."

"Do you understand what I'm saying?" I asked, starting

to get frustrated. Tess is so soft and delicate about everything that sometimes it seems like she's not *there*. I wanted to shake her. "She made the videos we saw on Viewer on Thursday night! We might be able to solve the mystery of where she is if we just figure out—"

"Solve the . . . *mystery*?" Tess interrupted defensively, putting her hands on her hips.

I quickly corrected myself. "I mean we might be able to find her."

Tess let it go, but said instead, "Frankie, the videos say they were added to Viewer two *years* ago."

"I know, that's what Officer Rollins said when I told him. But I think that—"

"You talked to Officer Rollins?" Tess interrupted.

"Will you stop interrupting me!" I shouted at her. She wrapped her long arms around her lanky body and pursed her lips. "I know the dates on the videos are wrong! I have a gut feeling that we need to pay attention to them!"

Tess stared at me for a second, then said quietly, "Frankie, the *police* are looking for her. They know what they're doing. And the dates on the videos aren't wrong."

"Don't you want to just *try*?" I asked. "Don't you want to do something other than sitting around with *Mia*?"

"Why'd you say Mia's name like that?" Tess asked, raising her eyebrows. "She's so nice! What's she ever done to you?"

"Are you serious?!" I shouted.

"Frankie, be quiet," Tess whispered. "One of the guests is going to call the front desk."

I was instantly furious, because Tess knew full well what Mia had done to me. "I don't care!" I screamed right in her face, standing on tiptoe to do it. Then, like a faucet had been turned on, tears gushed from my eyes.

"You are such a jerk," Tess said, stomping out the door but not slamming it, leaving me alone to cry.

I flopped, face-first, onto my bed and put a pillow over my head so I wouldn't get in trouble. Here's an embarrassing thing: the room I live in is double insulated for better soundproofing. My mom tried to have it done without me knowing, but I came home sick from school that day, so I know. Still, I buffered myself with my covers for an extra layer of sound protection because I really didn't want my mom to bring up going back on medication.

I don't need it!

I screamed over and over into the comforter, high-pitched, piercing my own eardrums. When I couldn't scream anymore, I continued to cry. Sometimes when I'm sad, all that my brain will think about is other sad things. It's like it wants to stay in a sad spiral. Today, feeling completely alone and misunderstood, I couldn't help but think about the day in February when Colette and I stopped being friends.

Colette, Tess, Mia, and some other girl in their math class were studying for a test. I came back from collecting shells at the beach and walked into my room, intending to go see if the others were done studying and wanted to hang out. The connecting door between my room and Tess's was open a little, so I could hear their conversation.

"Where's your sister?" Mia asked. I froze in the middle of my room, ears perking up.

"Uh . . . at the beach," Tess answered, her voice preoccupied. I couldn't see her but could picture her in her glasses reading her practice test intently.

"Doesn't she need to study, too?" Mia asked.

No, I thought to myself. *I know how to do geometry.*

"She doesn't really study unless our mom makes her," Tess said. I wanted to creep closer but was afraid the floorboards would creak and announce that I was listening. The door opened and someone else came into Tess's room and I thought: *Great! More people to talk about me!*

"Maybe her tests are just easier," Colette said.

"What do you mean?" some girl I didn't know asked.

"She gets to take them in a special room with just a couple other kids and wear headphones if she wants." Colette was spilling my secrets as if they were nothing, which felt like a slap in the face. And she wasn't even completely telling the truth. I didn't always take tests in different rooms, just sometimes . . . big tests. And I never used the head-phones because gross, who knew how many other kids had smashed their earwax against them?

"Maybe her class is just easier," the other girl said.

I made a face that said: *What the heck? No, it is not!*

I could feel the hotness in my cheeks and waited for Tess to stand up for me, to say that no, my math class was not easier than theirs. That my work was exactly the same. That even if I took a test in a smaller group sometimes, it was still the same test that they got.

I realized I was clenching my fists so tightly that I was digging my nails into my palms. And the conversation didn't stop there.

"Can you imagine Frankie taking this test?" Colette went on. "The question would ask her to calculate the volume of a rectangle and she'd write something about her favorite music. Get it, volume? The way she thinks about things is so random."

"Don't forget about her obsession with tornadoes," Mia said. "She's a total tornado brain."

All the voices that mattered in the world burst into laughter while my heart shattered into pieces. Tears pushed their way out of my eyes and down my hot cheeks; I wiped them away fiercely, so angry and hurt that Colette, my sup-posed best friend, would say those things. That Tess, my own twin sister, wouldn't defend me. Blood was pounding in my ears, making me tune out whatever came next. I needed to leave; I couldn't listen anymore. Silent as a spy on a mission, I left my room and crept away.

The next day was when I stopped taking my medication—without telling my mom at first. And the next week was when I started skipping my appointments with Gabe and hiding from the specialist at school. I wanted to show them all that I was normal just like them.

"I'm normal," I sobbed into my pillow. "I'm normal . . . I'm normal . . . I'm normal . . . I'm normal . . . I'm normal . . . I'm normal . . . I'm normal . . . I'm normal . . . I'm normal . . . I'm normal . . . I'm normal . . . I'm normal . . . I'm normal."

Repeating it didn't help me believe it: it just made the words loop together and sound funny and distract me from my sadness.

And just like that, the tears stopped.

chapter 12

Myth: Green clouds always tell you
that a tornado is forming.

AROUND THREE IN the afternoon, I decided to go out to the beach even though a storm was coming. It wasn't raining yet and the wind would feel nice on my puffy face. I put a windbreaker over my hoodie and left my room, looking sadly at Tess's door from the hallway as I went by.

I crunched across the parking lot, then sank deep into the squishy mountains of sand that made walking feel more like trudging. I didn't mind, though. With the crash of the ocean in my ears, I was immediately calmer and clearer than I'd been when I was cooped up indoors. At the edge of the water, it was windier without the protection of the dunes and my hair covered my face completely until I turned into the wind. There were dark gray clouds looming in the distance, so gray they almost looked green. Or maybe that was my imagination.

Inhaling the sea air, I got out my phone and looked through the four videos on our Viewer account again. It was weird that there were only four. We'd done so many dares—and we'd made videos of everything. With those plus the times Colette or Tess had scared each other (I stuck to dares), we should have had way more videos.

I rewatched the staring-at-Jake video, then the flowers-on-the-porch video. I watched one I hadn't seen before since it was on the second page of the account. It was a video of Colette singing. Her surroundings looked familiar, but I didn't know where she was at first. I wished she'd recorded with sound so I could hear the lyrics.

I made a fresh path of footprints as I watched the videos over and over. When I got to the running-in-beach-grass video the third time, I saw something I hadn't before: whale bones.

From where I was standing, I only had to turn my head to the right to see the whale bones display. Up on a bluff, the wood carvings of mother and baby gray whales were supported at their bellies by metal rods buried in the ground so the whales looked like they were swimming above the sand. The wood versions had replaced an actual whale skeleton when I was a little kid, but everyone still called the new wooden display whale bones. I guess the real skeleton was from a whale that'd washed up on the beach one time. Poor whale.

In the video Colette had made of her running feet, I could see the profile of the mother whale, and the water beyond.

I went over to the highest point of the bluff, then walked around in wide circles, looking at different angles. Behind me to the right, two police officers waded through the brush under the boardwalk, shining flashlights into the space beneath where a person could be hiding . . . or . . . I didn't want to think about that, so I focused on the whale bones.

"This is where the camera was," I murmured to myself, pointing to the ground.

There was a rock the size of a cantaloupe to the left side of the path. I wondered if Colette had put that rock there. I pictured her propping up the camera, hitting record, then running by, filming her feet and everything else the wide-angle caught.

I watched the waves crash, growing feistier with the brewing storm. Every time the sea pulled back, the pipers ran out to try to find food before the tide rolled back in. The seagulls squawked, cars bumped along the sandy roadway, and a family posed for a picture with the irritable ocean as the backdrop.

I tried to imagine Colette here, running past a camera

propped on a rock. I tried not to imagine where Colette was right now, where she'd been all night when everyone else had been sleeping in their warm beds.

You were out alone without friends or parents—just like the Sea Witch warned me about. A chill raced up my spine.

"What are you doing?"

I jumped.

"Don't sneak up on me!" I snapped, folding my arms over my chest. Tess had on a red windbreaker identical to mine. Sometimes our mom got things on sale and bought two of them. I kind of liked when we ended up in the same clothes, but I don't think Tess did.

"Sorry," she said easily. That word was harder for me to say than it seemed to be for her. "What are you doing out here?"

"This is where Colette did the running dare," I said. "Thursday night," I added for emphasis; it was still stinging that Tess didn't believe me. I faced the water and focused on staying calm with the ocean's help. A piece of my hair tickled my nose; I tucked it away. "I can't figure out which dare she was doing—since she was alone, it only showed her feet and the background. Maybe it was the one where you had to jump off the dune."

"I never liked that dare," Tess said. "I always worried I was going to get hurt. Or that you guys would."

You worry about everything, I thought but didn't say.

"Hey, Frankie, I'm not here to fight," Tess said. "I wanted to say sorry for calling you a jerk." She reached out like she was going to touch my shoulder but then didn't. I touched my other shoulder to balance myself out anyway.

"Okay."

"I shouldn't have said it, especially today, when you got your first—"

"Okay!" I cut her off. "I don't want to talk about that. Ever!"

She nodded, then continued. "I'm sorry for another thing, too. When Mia was in my room, we noticed that my clock was set to the wrong time." I stared at the ocean; she went on. "Remember that we just had daylight saving time a few weeks ago?"

"Huh?" I asked. I had no clue what she was talking about. I yanked out a piece of beach grass and started twirling it around my finger. It makes me feel better if my body is doing something, not just standing still.

"My clock," she explained. "I guess I forgot to set it forward when daylight saving time happened because I always just use the alarm on my phone. That's why I said that Colette came to my room at the same time you said she was in yours."

"So I was right," I said quietly.

"Yes, you were right," Tess admitted. "And I'm sorry. For both of those things."

"It's fine," I said. My finger was turning purple from the beach grass wound tightly around it. "It doesn't matter."

"It matters to me when I make mistakes. I mean, I told the police the wrong time. I could have completely messed them up."

"I don't think it was that big of a deal," I said, because now that I wasn't mad at her anymore, I could see that it wasn't. Sure, I wasn't the one who'd made the mistake, but forgetting to change your clock isn't the end of the world. I wanted to say that to Tess, but I didn't because I didn't think she would listen to me.

She was wandering through the grass, looking at the path.

"I did get hurt when I did that dare," Tess said quietly. "I twisted my ankle." Her mood-ring eyes were more green than gray or gold right then.

I nodded, remembering. We'd gone to the arcade earlier that day and played air hockey, then squished into the photo booth like sardines. I still had the picture strip somewhere. I'd made silly faces in all four pictures; Tess had smiled the same way in all of them; and Colette had posed like a model, blowing kisses or baring her shoulder.

"Maybe Colette was doing the dares as a surprise to you or something," I said. "Like as a funny present."

"Frankie, don't get mad at me for saying this, but the videos are old. They're from two years ago. I'm sure she was just messing around back then and we happened to see them now."

"But she made the one in Marsh's Thursday night," I said, breathing deeply to try to keep myself in check. "Kai told me."

"Kai told you that she made *a* video that night, not necessarily *that* video that's on Viewer," Tess said.

"He said her hair was the same," I said.

"She's worn her hair in knots like that since we were little, Frankie," Tess said. "The videos are old."

If your brain twists and turns like mine, it's easy to get confused when people tell you you're definitively wrong. Watching the seagulls struggle to fly in the building wind, I began to question what I was saying. I got out my phone and scrolled through the videos again.

I noticed something about one of them.

"Tess!" I said, turning to face her. "Colette's singing in the gym at school in this one. I didn't recognize where it was at first, but that's where it is, see?" I shoved my phone at her, and she stepped in to look.

"You didn't show me this one," she said, taking my phone and watching. "I wish we could hear what she's singing. I wonder if it's that song—" Tess gasped, making me jump.

"What?" I asked, annoyed at being startled.

"Ohmygod, Frankie, I think you're right!" she said, eyes

wide. "I think you're actually right that she made these videos Thursday night—or at least recently."

I couldn't help myself: I grabbed back the phone to see if I could understand why Tess had flipped the switch from practically telling me I was a liar to agreeing with me so quickly. I stared at the phone, but it looked the same to me.

"She's wearing the scarf she borrowed from me," Tess said.

"So?" I asked.

"So she borrowed it on Thursday night!" Tess said excitedly. "She had to have made this that night!"

"Let's go look at the school!" I said. "Maybe there's a clue that will help us remember more of the dares. I really think that if we figure out what she was doing, we can help find her."

"You're being really . . . you're . . ." Tess began, then paused for a few seconds. "You're doing a nice thing for her, but you and Colette haven't been exactly . . ."

She didn't have to say it; I didn't want her to.

"Just because you think someone sucks doesn't mean you want bad things to happen to them," I said.

Tess nodded slowly.

"Honestly, I think the police are our best hope," she said. "But you were right earlier that trying is better than sitting around stressing out." She smiled a little. "Let's see if the school makes us remember anything else." Ready to go, I started down the path toward the street; she grabbed my arm and I pulled it away, thinking, but not saying, *Don't touch me.* "We're only doing this until dinner, okay? It'll be getting dark after that."

"So?"

"So I don't want to be out in the dark."

That was surprising to hear since Tess had never been afraid of the dark before. In fact, all our lives, she was the one who *wanted* to go out at night.

"Fine by me," I said, feeling unsettled by the change in Tess.

We plodded down the dune.

"Can I tell you a secret?" Tess asked as we trudged through the divots at exactly the same pace. She didn't wait for me to say yes. "Colette came to my room to ask for the scarf, but while she was there, she told me something terrible. Her parents are making her move to Seattle after school gets out. I guess her dad got a new job. She said she doesn't want to go and they got in a big fight about it and she stormed out of the house without telling them where she was going. She was really upset. She asked me to get her some cucumber water to calm her down, but she was gone when I came back."

"Wow," I said.

"You can't tell anyone," Tess said. "Mia doesn't know."

"Why didn't you tell her?" I asked, my chest full in a good way because I had been told something that others hadn't heard.

Tess shrugged. "You know how she is. I mean, she's fun to be around, but she can't keep a secret." She paused. "I told the police, but they already knew because Colette's parents told them about it."

"Tess?"

"Yeah?"

"Maybe Colette really was making you a present with the dare videos," I said. "But not a funny one, more a sentimental one." I hesitated, then added, "More of a goodbye present."

She tucked her hair back. There was a little knot in her hair under her ear like she'd been twisting it. "I guess that's possible," she said quietly. Then, because maybe that possibility stressed her out, she started biting the nail of her middle finger as we walked, in sync, toward school.

chapter 13

Fact: It's possible to have a tornado
and a hurricane at the same time.

TESS AND I stared up at the two-story redbrick building
where we spent so much of our time: Ocean View Middle
School.

"What time is it?" Tess asked, her arms wrapped around
her middle, hunching over. I don't know why some tall girls
do that. I wouldn't: I'd stand up straight and touch the ceiling to see how it feels.

"Four fifteen," I said, putting my cell back in my pocket.

"Maybe this is a bad idea. We could get in trouble."

"We won't," I said casually.

"I'm seriously so nervous right now," Tess said, biting
her nail. "I feel like I'm going to have a panic attack."

"You won't," I said, because she had never had one.

"How are you not nervous?"

I shrugged. "I don't get nervous."

Sometimes I think that twins get unequal traits, like one gets all of something and the other gets none of it. Tess got all the nervousness and artistic ability and niceness and I got all the . . . I don't know what I got.

Not wanting to think about that, I walked up to the front door of the school and yanked it open.

Tess's eyes widened. "It's unlocked?"

"Some of the teachers work weekends," I said, shrugging again.

"How did you know that?"

"Because of when I did that Saturday kite-making class."

"What if they see us?" Tess asked, looking completely freaked out. I didn't know how someone who loved haunted houses thought going into our school on a Saturday afternoon was so terrifying.

"We could say we forgot a book or something?"

"How did you think of that so quickly?" She was still frozen outside the door.

"I just did," I said impatiently. "Are you coming or not?"

"Ohmygod," Tess whispered as she walked through the door I was holding open. I followed her in. She looked down the hall to the left, then the right. "I don't see anyone."

"Good! Let's go!"

I started walking down the main hall toward the lockers for our grade. The gym where Colette had made the singing-dare video was just beyond our lockers. Tess followed me instead of walking next to me. Once she and Colette tricked me into watching a horror movie where the girl who went last got killed first: I didn't remind Tess of that. She didn't seem in the mood to be scared—any more than she already was. We went by classroom after classroom and they all had their lights off. They weren't dark—just dim—because it was still light out, and they all had windows. The storm clouds had cleared.

"Maybe Principal Golden's here," I said.

"I hope not!" Tess whispered.

"When did you turn into such a scaredy-cat?" I said. This wasn't normal for Tess.

"Shhh!" she whispered. "Be quiet!"

"No one's in the hallway," I said in my regular voice.

"Frankie, stop it!"

"Fine," I groaned, walking in silence for a few minutes. But then, without warning, I became very aware of my socks crowding and tickling my feet inside my shoes; the scratchiness of the tag in my sweatshirt at the back of my neck; the elastic gripping my wrists. There was only one surefire way to get my mind off my grippy, prickly clothing:

To run.

I bolted, pounding my feet hard against the floor all the way down the hall, shaking my wrists as I went. Some person called an occupational therapist had told me to try running once when I was having a supersensory freak-out moment. It worked, so I do it when I can—not in the middle of class or something.

I didn't stop until I reached the beginning of the locker bank. I doubled over and rested my hands on my knees, slowing my breath until Tess caught up.

"Did it work?" she asked.

I stood up straight and nodded once, brushing my bangs out of my eyes.

"Your hair looks cute," Tess said, tilting her head to the side. "The curls are less, uh . . ."

"Frizzy?" I asked, frowning.

She opened her mouth to answer but her phone buzzed and startled us both, making me jump and making her squeal like a mouse. I frowned deeper at being scared, but Tess burst into hysterical laughter because she loves watching other people freak out in fear. I couldn't help but laugh a little, too.

When we calmed down, Tess pulled out her phone and checked it.

"Is it Mom?" I asked, stepping closer to look over her shoulder.

"No, it's Mia," Tess said, reading the text. I moved away quickly while Tess kept talking. "She's back at her house, worrying about Colette. I mean, we all are. I should probably tell her what we think she was do—"

"No!" I shouted. Tess looked at me, surprised. In a lower voice, I said, "Mia's not a part of this. She never was."

When Mia had shown up in the middle of last year, Tess and Colette were fascinated by her mainly because she'd moved here from New York. At least that's what I thought at first. But then Tess and Mia had art class together, and Tess thought Mia's paintings were beautiful and her jokes were hilarious. Mia's big personality is basically the exact opposite of Tess's reserved one—and I guess Tess liked that.

And Colette got obsessed with Mia's stories about riding the subway and seeing celebrities on the street corners and Mia's general coolness. Tess was just friends with her, but Colette seemed to kind of idolize Mia.

But what my sister and my former best friend never noticed while they were friending or idolizing her was that Mia just didn't *get* me. It was obvious. And because of that, our friend group changed.

So much that I wasn't a part of it anymore.

Tess pursed her lips like Mom did sometimes. "I don't understand why you hate her so much."

"I don't get why you *like* her so much." *Especially since she turned Colette into a total backstabber who said terrible things about your sister,* I thought but didn't say.

Tess sighed loudly but put away her phone without replying to Mia's text. She flipped around and went over to her locker. As she was doing the combination, she said, "I don't say bad stuff about *your* friends."

"What friends?" I muttered, wanting to tell her that, by not standing up for me, she'd taken my single friend away. I mean, Tess could have made Colette understand that she'd been wrong. She could have helped Mia get to know me, maybe. Instead, Tess had gone along with the mean stuff Colette and Mia said by not saying anything. Her silence had told them it was okay.

I didn't want to think about that anymore. "Why are you opening your locker?" I asked my sister. "Let's go to the gym."

"Because I want to show you something."

Tess flung open the locker door. I walked over and stood behind her, peering in. It looked like a normal locker—well, normal for Tess and Colette. There was a magnetic mirror stuck to the back of the door surrounded by a bunch of photos taped up with emoji washi tape.

There was a shelf that split the guts of the locker in half and I could tell which part belonged to which girl immediately. On top, the books and binders stood vertically in a row, neatly organized and looking like they were issued yesterday. That was signature Tess. On the bottom, books, loose papers, and tattered folders with drawings all over them were layered in an organized mess, which was Colette in a nutshell.

"Look," Tess said, pointing at the picture collage that covered the entire inside of the locker door.

"What?" I asked.

"Look at the pictures," Tess said.

"What about them?" I asked, not getting what she was saying.

Tess rolled her eyes. "You're in them, Frankie," she said. I took a closer look and she was right: I was in at least a dozen of them.

"What's your point?" I asked, stepping away.

"Just that even though you and Colette were fighting or whatever, she never took down the pictures of you."

I thought about that, and the naturally skeptical side of me said, "That's because she shares a locker with my sister."

Tess ignored that comment, touching a picture of Colette. In it, Colette was smiling huge, jumping off something so her red hair was flying out in all directions. "I hope she's okay."

"Are you crying?" I asked, leaning around to look at her. Her eyes looked like tiny buckets.

"It's just . . . seeing her face," Tess said. "I'm really worried about her, Frankie." Tess looked at me with big, sad eyes and it made my heart pinch. "What if no one finds her?"

"We're going to," I said. "Will you get out a piece of paper and pencil?"

Tess nodded and handed me a notebook with a pen stuck in the spiral. I sat down on the floor, leaning against the wall on the opposite side of the hall, stretching out my legs in front of me. When I did, Tess slid to the floor, too, stretching her legs out like a mirror of mine. The bottoms of our feet were only about a foot apart.

In the notebook, I wrote which dares Colette had done from dare-or-scare recently:

Running off dune dare?
Ding-dong-ditch . . . but with flowers.
Singing in public (gym).
Staring at something gross (Jake).

"We need to remember more of the dares," I said, eyes on the page. "I think it's important. I'll bring this with us." I started to rip out the paper. "And we can write down our notes. Can I borrow the pen?"

I reached across and handed the notebook back to Tess. She looked like she'd been blasted off to space while I was making the list. "What's wrong?" I asked.

"Do you think she killed herself and wants us to find her?"

The words made my heart jump. It felt like too big a thing to say out loud, let alone think about.

"No!" I said. Then, "She better not have!"

"It happens," spacey Tess said. "I read a book about it. You can think someone is completely fine and then they kill themselves. I mean, she *had* gotten into a fight with her parents. She was really upset about the idea of moving to Seattle."

"You should read happier books," I said. Then, rationally, I added, "People kill themselves because they have depression, not because of a single fight."

"How do you know so much about it?"

"I saw a book at Gabe's office once." The conversation was making me feel on edge. I was starting to notice my restrictive clothes again. "Do you think she's depressed?"

"No," Tess admitted. "I don't really know what that means, but I don't think so."

I didn't really either, and I didn't *want* to know. "Stop talking about that."

"Okay," she said, her voice a little more normal.

"Are *you* depressed?" I asked.

"No!" she said strongly, looking at me funny. "Are you?"

"No?" I said like a question, looking at her funny right back. "How do you know if you're depressed?"

I wondered if depression was something you caught like the flu or Ebola and you didn't know you had it until it was too late.

"You're the one who read a book about it!" Tess said.

"I didn't read it cover to cover," I said. "I didn't memorize it! I just flipped through it." Then, "Let's seriously stop talking about this."

"Okay," Tess said. She folded her legs into crisscross applesauce. "But if you ever feel, like, um . . . bad . . . you know you can . . ."

"I know." Awkward pause. "You too."

"I mean because friendships can be—"

"Don't talk about that either." I cut her off, looking back at the paper again. I drew a tornado in the corner, then another one, then another one. Without the notebook under the paper, the pen poked through and made marks on my jeans.

"Let's just get back to dare-or-scare," I said, standing up. "Let's go to the gym and—"

A door slammed with a *boom* at the other end of the main hall. Tess and I both looked toward the sound, then back at each other, eyes wide. She stood up fast.

"Come on," I said in a low voice, pointing toward the gym, which happened to be in the opposite direction of where the sound had come from. "We can go out that way."

We ran down the hall and pushed through the double doors to the gym as quietly as we could, our sneakers squeaking against the shiny floor as we hurried toward the door leading out.

When we were almost there, I turned back to look at the wide-open space. "Where did she make the video?" I asked, pulling out my phone and unlocking it. The screen was still on the singing dare.

"What are you doing?" Tess asked. "Someone's coming; we have to go."

"We will," I said. "Just let me look really quick."

I held my phone out in front of my face and turned in a semicircle, trying to match the backgrounds here to the one in the video.

"She was right over there," I said, pointing. "Under the basket. See, you can see the edge of the poster in the video?"

"Frankie, we have to leave," Tess said, pulling on me.

"Stop!" I said. "I'm trying to concentrate!" But there was no way I could let my brain remember anything when I was being rushed and pulled by Tess. I needed her to be quiet and leave me alone, but she wouldn't. I was starting to get mad. "Stop touching me!"

"Stop yelling at me!" Tess yelled herself. "I'm leaving, and you should, too. We are going to get in trouble, Frankie. This is really stupid!"

"Don't call me stupid!" I shouted, my throat tightening, my cheeks growing hot.

"Ugh!" Tess shouted, frustrated. "I didn't say that!"

"Just leave and go hang out with Mia," I said nastily. "I know that's where you'd rather be."

"I should," Tess said. "At least she doesn't yell at me all the time. I swear, I don't know why you take everything out on me! And you're so mean to Mia for no reason!"

That was it.

I put my phone away and flipped around, hands clenched into fists, the storm rising up from my belly, growing stronger with every vertebra it passed. When it finally reached my mouth, it'd turned into an EF5-caliber issue.

"I hate her!" I screamed, my words echoing off the walls of the huge space. Tess looked like she'd been slapped.

"You have no reason to hate her!" Tess screamed back, looking angrier than I'd ever seen her. We were two storms colliding.

"I have a great reason!" I shouted. "She turned Colette against me! She's a snake and she made Colette one, too. They talked about me behind my back and made fun of me and . . ." I sniffed to try to control the river of tears. "And thanks for standing up for me, by the way! I thought sisters were supposed to be there for each other!"

In a flash, Tess didn't look angry anymore. Instead, she looked shocked, her eyebrows up and her mouth open a little. I turned around and walked toward the door leading outside.

"Wait, Frankie," Tess said, following me. "I don't know what you're talk—"

"Hey, you kids!" the janitor shouted. In normal school hours, he was perfectly harmless. Now he was sweaty, angry, and scary. "You're not supposed to be in here!"

I bolted through the door, and a few seconds later, Tess was outside, too. It was still light out, but the sun was closer to the beach now. The cloudy sky and long shadows gave the town an eerie filter as we ran across the street, through the mini-carnival, down Pacific, past the go-karts and horses, and into the inn's parking lot. The only sounds I could hear were the slaps of our shoes on pavement and the blood pumping in my ears. Pirate was lying under the bench in the covered outdoor area; she raised an eyebrow at me.

"Tell Mom . . . ," I gasped, "I'm sick . . ." I sucked in air. "And I don't want dinner."

I took off running toward the beach. Pirate barked, keeping up with me, her tags going *tink-tink* as she trotted along.

"Wait, Frankie!" Tess called again before I was out of earshot.

I didn't stop: I couldn't be inside. I ran toward the ocean until my feet and pant legs were soaked, and when a huge gust of wind barreled through, I screamed the loudest I ever have in my life.

chapter 14

Fact: Some animals seem to sense when weather disturbances like tornadoes are about to happen.

PIRATE HAD FOLLOWED me. She must have just known I needed a friend. I should have been going to the cottage for dinner, but instead, I walked along the shore with Pirate by my side, then planted myself on a huge log. It was closer to the dune than to the water, which meant it was more sheltered. Pirate lay at my feet and we watched a runner near the surf lean into the wind as she went by almost in slow motion, her hair blown back like she was coming up from underwater.

The waves were so choppy now that the tide was leaving huge, frothy mounds of bubbles on the sand. Then the wind blew the mounds along, and they looked like miniature icebergs. I zoned out, staring at one point, seeing the movement of the waves and the icebergs and the pipers all around in my peripheral vision.

The ocean made me feel calm. It had since the first time I'd seen it. I forget things sometimes, but I haven't forgotten the first time we came here.

Mom picked us up on the last day of preschool with the trunk packed with so much stuff, my artwork and desk supplies had no place to go but under my feet.

"We're going on an adventure!" Mom said when we were buckled up.

"Where are we going?" Tess asked.

"We're going to the beach!" Mom said, but she didn't seem excited. It wasn't sunny out, but she was wearing sunglasses.

"The beach!" I shouted, thinking it'd be like the roped-off sandy area by the small lake near our house. "Yay!"

"When are we coming back?" Tess asked.

"We'll see," Mom said, pulling out of the parking lot. "How would you guys like to watch a show? I put your devices and headphones in the seat pockets."

When we arrived after our five-hour ride, Mom stopped the car under the WORLD'S LONGEST BEACH sign and made us take off our headphones. Normally, I would have protested, but the sight of the ocean was distracting, and if you tell me something is the world's best or longest or tallest something, I get curious.

"Look what we can do!" Mom said before she pushed the gas pedal and drove out onto the sand. "We can drive right on the beach! Isn't this great?"

The drier sand yanked the car back and forth and the bumps made us jump in our seats. Mom rolled down all four windows and the sea air whipped our hair around the car. We made a left onto the packed wet sand and Mom drove along with the waves coming right up to kiss our tires.

"I love it here," I said after only being in Long Beach about five minutes. Already, in preschool, the world felt daunting to me. I could tell right away that the beach would be a place that would make it a little less so.

"I'm scared," Tess said, reaching over and grabbing my hand. "What if we drive under the water?"

"Then we'll meet a narwhal," I said, putting my free hand out of the car to surf on the wind. I loved that feeling.

"Can we go back on the normal road, Mommy?" Tess asked.

"I want to stay on the beach!" I said. "I want to live on the beach."

Mom pulled over and parked the car on the dry sand, so the front windshield was facing away from the ocean and toward a four-story building. It had huge windows looking out toward the water, reflecting it back. Mom turned around and took off her sunglasses. Her eyes were red and tired, but she was smiling.

"You can't live right on the beach, Frankie," she said, "but is that close enough?" She pointed at the building.

"We get to live there?" I asked in disbelief.

Mom nodded. "It's an inn, which is like a hotel. I've been offered a job as the manager. For as long as I work at the inn, we get to live in that little cottage over there." She beamed at us. "Then we can come to the beach every single day."

"Where's Ronan?" Tess asked. "Is he coming, too?"

Ronan was Mom's boyfriend before Charles. I barely remember him: when I think of him, he has a blurry face. I don't think he was very nice to my mom.

"Remember our talk last week?" Mom asked. "Remember what I said about Ronan's mistake and us moving out?"

"Can I go play on the beach?" I interrupted because I didn't want to hear the story again. She said I could, and I went and chased pipers.

Lost in thought about the day we'd arrived, I didn't hear someone come up behind me—but Pirate let me know: her tags *tink-tinked* when she raised her head to look.

" 'Sup, Frank and Beans," Kai said. I turned around and looked at him standing there with his skateboard in his hand, still wearing his yellow beanie, the sunset turning his face even more golden than it usually was. I'm not going to lie: it made me feel squishy like a sand mountain.

"Hi," I said.

"Shove over," he said, coming around the log to sit down

with me. I moved as far away as possible without falling onto the sand. "What're you doing out here? My dad's convinced it's going to storm. Hey, Pirate," he said, scratching her head.

"Nothing," I said, because that sounded better than telling him I was recovering from an epic meltdown. "Looks like your mom let you out of the shop."

"Finally," he groaned.

Pirate jumped up on Kai's knees and started licking his face; I liked that he just let her and didn't gross out. Pirate knew not to do that to me because I *would* gross out: I can't help it. Kai just laughed, rubbing her ears with both hands. When he asked, "Who's a good girl?" Pirate smiled at him.

He looked over at me with his nice eyes and good eyebrows. My heartbeat sped up and my hands felt clammy. Maybe I could feel nervous after all! I wanted to tell Tess, but then I remembered I was mad at her.

Kai was still staring at me.

"What?" I asked him, looking back at the ocean so he'd hopefully do the same.

"You didn't write me back earlier," he said. "Did you see my texts?"

"I didn't get any," I said, pulling out my phone, thankful for something to do. After I'd looked at Viewer so many times earlier and not closed the app, the battery on my phone had taken a hit. "It's dead," I said, holding it up as if he could see the tiny battery icon from all the way on the other side of the log. "Why'd you text me?"

"To tell you I remembered something about when Colette came to the store," he said. Pirate settled down on his feet, and Kai kept petting her.

"What did you remember?" I asked excitedly.

"Nothing, just that she asked me where the Sea Witch lives."

I sucked in my breath. "What?" All at once, my body went crazy, my heart jumping hurdles, my neck turning hot, the place where the Sea Witch had grabbed my wrist sending a twinge of pain.

Colette had asked where the Sea Witch lived.

I'd seen the Sea Witch at the police station.

Did the Sea Witch have Colette?

"Why did she want to know *that*?" I managed to ask Kai.

"Dunno," he said super-casually. It made me want to scream and shake him—but then I'd have to touch him.

"She literally asked you for the Sea Witch's address?" I blinked a bunch, as if it would clear up my confusion.

"No, she literally asked for the address of the person with the stuffed animals in their yard," Kai said. "I told her that person was the Sea Witch. *Then* she asked for the Sea Witch's address."

"But why . . ." My mind raced. *Why did . . . what would . . .*

but how ... and when ... ? "Wait." I looked at Kai. "Why did she ask *you* that?"

"Ask me what?" Kai and Pirate were in their own world.

"Why did Colette ask you where the Sea Witch lives?" I shouted. "How the heck do you know that?"

"Whoa, calm your status, Franklin," Kai said good-naturedly. "She buys those weird taxidermy animals my parents sell. She has a collection, I guess. They're too big and heavy for her to take home herself, so she has them delivered." Kai pulled out his phone and scrolled through for a second. Then he showed me a picture of a notecard with a name and address written on it. "See? I sent it to you."

Leaning over to look, I shivered, still phantom-feeling the Sea Witch's fingers wrapped around my wrist. The name on the card said *Mikayla Sievich*.

"See-vich," I murmured, then it hit me. "Is that where she got the nickname? From her last name?"

"I guess so. And because she's such a witch to all the kids in town. She stuck a knife in Dillon's soccer ball once. For real."

"Uh-huh," I said, not totally listening to him. I was too focused on the Sea Witch's warning: *You never know what may happen to bad children running around with no parents.*

Had the Sea Witch done something to Colette?

Kai cleared his throat. "Hey, that sucks that no one else believes you about when Colette made the videos."

"Uh-huh," I said, still more preoccupied by the conversation I was having inside my head.

"I mean, since you can choose the upload date," he said.

My head snapped in his direction. "What?" I shouted. "Why are you just casually telling me all of these important things?!"

"You didn't know that?" he asked.

"No, because you didn't tell me!" I shouted.

He laughed, which might have bugged me if I thought that he was laughing at me in a mean sense. But Kai's not like that.

"Okay!" he said. "So yeah, you can set your upload date to whatever you want. It'll use the current date automatically, or you can change it to anything. Even the future."

"How do you know that? Are you sure?"

"I've done it," he said, nodding. "For the edits that me and Dillon make sometimes of us doing board tricks and stuff."

"But why say a video was uploaded on a different day than when it was?" I seriously could not believe that he hadn't told me this until now.

"Dunno why other people would want to," Kai said, "but Dillon has this thing about only posting on our channel on Thursdays. He says, like, people will get more excited to see our board tricks if they have to wait a few days for them." Kai shook his hair out of his eyes and added, "It's lame because we only have seven followers, but whatever. The only problem is if he puts a video on our account with a date from the past, it doesn't hit me up that there's a new video . . . so I don't see it."

"Wait, so you mean that if you make a video on a Friday, you can upload it but change the date to the day before, a Thursday?"

"Yup."

"Or you could upload a video today but change the date to say it was uploaded two years ago?" I asked, trying to understand what Kai was telling me.

"Yup yup," he said.

"And if you did that, people wouldn't get a notification that a new video was uploaded . . . because the date was in the past?"

"You got it," Kai said before cracking up. "Oh man, one time I wiped out *extra* in a video that Dillon posted with a different date. My sister obsessively checks the channel because she has a crush on Dillon, and she saw it and was making fun of me, and I didn't even know what she was talking about to defend myself . . ."

My thoughts were on a Tilt-A-Whirl: changing video-upload dates, Colette making the videos again, Colette asking Kai about the Sea Witch, the Sea Witch being at the police station. The warning.

"I have to find Tess," I said, interrupting whatever Kai

was saying about his epic wipeout. He looked bummed, which I noticed, which I felt proud for noticing, so I forced myself to use the hard word. "Sorry for interrupting you."

"S'okay," Kai said, standing up and brushing the sand off his jeans. "I gotta go anyway; we're going to a movie." He stretched like he'd just gotten up from a nap and looked off to the right, toward the inn. "Oh, hey, you don't need to go far to find your sister. She's coming this way."

Kai and Tess waved at each other, but Kai didn't wait for her to reach the log before he left. I thanked him for the information and tried not to feel sad that he was leaving.

"There you are," Tess said, crunching closer through the sand.

She sat down on the log next to me, but leaving space between us, shivering and pulling her jacket tighter. My log was getting a lot of traffic.

"Frankie, will you please tell me what Colette and Mia did—why you're so mad?" Tess asked.

"I don't want to talk about it," I said quickly. I really didn't, but not because it was painful or because I thought we'd fight again. Well, that stuff, too. But more because I wanted to get all of the other stuff in my brain out of my mouth, so she'd help me figure it out.

Everything except the Sea Witch's warning. For some reason, I wanted to keep that to myself. Maybe I thought it would scare Tess too much—and she was being weird about being scared today. Maybe I thought she'd brush it off like she had with my earlier ideas, when she didn't believe me about Colette making the dare videos recently. Maybe I just wanted to know something that no one else did.

"That's what you've been telling me for months—that you don't want to talk about it," Tess was saying, "but that thing you said in the gym about me not . . . sticking up for you? I don't know what you mean." She paused, then added, "I even called Mia and asked her about it." I looked at her, surprised. "She said she didn't know what I meant, but I . . . I don't know. I feel like she was being weird. Will you please tell me what happened?"

"I'll tell you," I said, and she looked hopeful, "but not right now. Kai told me two things when he was here—and those things are more important than a fight."

"Do you promise we'll talk about it later, though?" Tess asked. And somehow, her caring enough to make me promise made my anger at her stay away. I nodded, and she smiled. "Okay, tell me what Kai said."

chapter 15

Opinion: *The Wizard of Oz* is probably the most
popular movie with a tornado in it ever.

"IS IT OKAY if Frankie and I go to a movie after dinner?"
Tess asked, looking at Mom with big innocent eyes. She was
sitting straight up in her chair and smiling a little, and I
made a mental note to practice that posture later. It seemed
to be effective, judging by the fact that Mom hadn't immediately said no.

"Together?" Mom asked. She looked at Charles and he
shrugged before blowing his nose with a huge honk in a
dinner napkin. *Gross.*

"Yes," Tess and I said at the same time.

"It *is* Saturday night," Tess said.

Mom narrowed her eyes at us. "Are you two up to
something?"

"We just want to go to a movie," Tess said. Then she

made her tone sound sad. "We just want a distraction. Watching a movie is good for that. There will be other kids there, too."

"That's understandable," Charles chimed in, his nose stuffy. "But because of Colette, it's hard to want to let you two go off on your own at night."

"Stop giving the dog crab," my mom snapped at him, frowning. "It's expensive."

"Sorry, Pirate," Charles said to the beggar by his side. "The lady of the house says you're cut off." He sneezed and I moved my chair away from his.

"We'll be careful," Tess promised. "Can we please go? It's only a few blocks away."

I stayed quiet, letting her handle the negotiations.

"I don't know about this," Mom said, looking at Charles. They stared at each other for like a whole minute, seeming to have a conversation telepathically. Finally Mom sighed and looked at us. "You'll walk there and back together?"

"Yes," Tess and I said in unison.

"And sit together?" Mom asked. "And keep your phones on vibrate?"

We both nodded enthusiastically.

"Which movie are you seeing?" Mom asked.

"The superhero one," Tess said. "It's PG-13."

"You don't like superhero movies," Mom said, eyeing me skeptically.

"This one looks good," I said. *Don't ask me the title. Don't ask me the title!*

"All right, you can go, but text when you get there, and be home by ten thirty," Mom said, giving in.

"The movie might not be over by then," Tess said innocently.

"Fine, eleven," Mom said. "And text when you leave to come home."

"We will," Tess said, nodding.

"Promise," I said.

———

WHEN WE SET out, it was completely dark. I rode behind Tess—in the horror-movie, get-killed-first spot—because she still seemed off about the dark. It wasn't so much that I minded riding in the dark, at least not yet, but I minded the change in Tess. I minded that *she* was afraid.

We rode in the middle of Ocean Beach Boulevard because that's where the lights from the houses on both sides of the streets shone the brightest. There aren't any sidewalks in the residential part of the town, and besides, you can see headlights coming from a mile away.

I followed the blinking light on the back of Tess's bike, talking a lot to keep myself from thinking a lot.

"Is it Seventeenth or Eighteenth?" I called to Tess. It was the third time I'd asked her.

"Eighteenth," Tess answered over her shoulder, her voice higher than usual. "Two more blocks."

"And what are we going to do when we get there?" I asked.

"This was your idea, Frankie," Tess said. "I don't know!"

"We'll just look," I said, trying to make myself feel better. "We can even look from pretty far away if we want."

My stomach did somersaults thinking about riding toward the Sea Witch instead of riding away from her as fast as I could like I wanted to. With every spin of the pedals, I dreaded where we were going more.

In front of me, Tess bumped over a pothole and I dodged it. I kept talking. "Remember when Colette hit that huge pothole that was completely obvious to everyone else but her and she went over her handlebars?"

Tess started laughing, which made me calm down a little. "Ohmygod, yes, she did a full flip in the air. She's the worst bike rider; she's so uncoordinated."

"And that sound she made . . . ," I said, laughing, too. "Yeeeeee-oooow!"

"I forgot about that!" Tess laughed harder. "She's so lucky she landed in grass."

Tess took the right on Eighteenth and I followed, making a wide arc, and the somersaults in my belly were back. Tess slowed down; I almost ran into her back tire, pedaling backward to brake fast since the cruiser didn't have a hand brake.

"Let's leave our bikes here," Tess whispered.

"Good idea," I whispered.

We walked the cruisers over to the side of the road and leaned them against someone's tree. It was low hanging, and I hoped no spiders would drop into my hair.

The big houses on this block were dark: they were probably vacation homes owned by people who didn't live in Long Beach all the time. It felt like they'd been abandoned.

"Maybe we should come back tomorrow," I whispered. My heart was racing and my mouth felt like I'd eaten sand.

"We're already here," Tess said, but she looked like a scared squirrel in a car's headlights. "Let's get it over with."

"Fine," I said. "Let's just go."

Crouched together, walking carefully, we approached a huge house with ten steep steps leading up to a shadowy porch. It didn't look anything like the porch in the ding-dong-ditch dare video, but it looked like a house where a witch would live. The roof jutted up to sharp points and the steps and house itself were solid brick and menacing. The mailbox said *Sievich* in faded, angry handwriting.

"It's not the same house in the video where Colette left the flowers," I whispered to Tess.

"How do you know?" she whispered back.

"Those were wooden steps, not brick. And they were wider."

"You noticed that?" she asked, scooting closer to me. I

shrugged. Sometimes I notice things. Sometimes I don't. It's like I'm always out of sync.

Or at least usually. Gabe tells me not to use "forever" words like *always*. And *forever*. He says they're almost *always* an exaggeration and exaggerations aren't a clear way to speak.

I missed Gabe.

Tess was talking. "Why did Colette want to come here if—"

"Listen," I interrupted. I thought I'd heard something, but when Tess and I stopped talking, there was nothing but the ocean in the distance and a wind chime tinkling on a porch nearby.

"Is that her driveway?" Tess asked, pointing to the gravel alley to the left of the house.

"Probably," I whispered. Tess started walking toward the driveway and I followed automatically because I didn't want to be alone in front of the Sea Witch's house. Of course I noticed that I was in get-killed-first position again. The trees were spooky black silhouettes. "This is a bad idea," I said, tiptoeing behind my sister on the gravel.

"Let me remind you: this was *your* idea," Tess whispered, stopping suddenly when we were all the way down the driveway. "Ohmygod."

"Holy guacamole," I said, blinking in the dim light from the outdoor lamps, taking in the yard. There were animals everywhere—dead, stuffed ones—all looking like they wanted to eat us alive. As I stared at a grizzly bear, some-thing important clicked into place.

I'd been here before—and I remembered why.

I turned toward the porch, which stretched the entire length of this side of the house. It didn't have any furniture, though, like no one ever sat out there, watching the sunset, listening to the waves. This side was covered in gray shin-gles, not brick, and had more windows than walls—every one of them dark. The house looked like two people with very different faces standing back-to-back: one guarding the street and one watching the ocean.

On this side, the steps up to the porch were wide and wooden. *These* were the steps in Colette's video.

"This was her combo dare!" I whispered to Tess. "Remember? Colette dared us to do something nice *and* daring at the same time. She left taffy that time, but she still did the ding-dong-ditch. You both did it!"

"You did it, too!" Tess said excitedly. "I had no idea it was the Sea Witch's house!"

"Me neither!" I said, horrified at the realization that Colette had come here on Thursday night to redo a dare from our childhood and might have been snatched by a crazy lady. "Do you think she's going to have Colette stuffed like one of her animals?"

"No!" Tess whispered. "Don't say that!"

Tess didn't know about the Sea Witch's warning, and I *definitely* wasn't going to tell her right then, tiptoeing between carcasses of a bobcat and a super-scary-looking bird. The hair on the back of my neck was standing up: a sensation I hated very much.

I looked in the direction of the beach, remembering approaching the house from that way. We'd leave our bikes on the bike path along the dunes and sneak through the huge lawn with little gifts, like pet rocks or taffy. Colette had chosen this house because she felt sorry for whoever lived here among all the dead animals. I wonder if she would have chosen it if she'd known who it belonged to.

"Why did she film this dare again?" Tess asked quietly. "And why the running one—and the singing-in-public one?" She laughed a little. "You wanted to avoid the scare part of dare-or-scare so bad that you were willing to do the singing dare, do you remember?"

I rolled my eyes but didn't answer.

Tess gripped my arm, making me jump. "Maybe she was just doing the dares all three of us did. Maybe she was making the videos as a goodbye present to both of us, Frankie!"

It was a nice thought, but my pessimistic side wouldn't let me believe that Colette had included me in this, especially since I'd yelled at her when she'd asked for Fred.

"I don't think so," I whispered. "Like you just said, I did

every single one of the dares because I didn't want to be scared."

"But I didn't," Tess said. "And Colette didn't. We liked the scares. It wouldn't be that many, honestly. I mean, think about it: All three of us did the dares she made videos of, right? You sang, did this"—she gestured behind her at the house—"jumped off the dune, and stared at Jake, right?"

"Yeah," I said. "I think so."

"So did I—and so did she," Tess said excitedly, her fear temporarily gone from her face. "We just need to figure out what other dares fit."

I was tired, and a feeling of sadness sank into my veins out of nowhere. I looked around the dark landscape and all at once wished I were at home, curled up, scrolling through the TwisterLvr feed like I usually do before bed. "Maybe this whole thing is stupid and neither of us should be here. Maybe I was wrong."

"We need to be here," Tess whispered. "*You* need to be here, not for Colette, but for me. I think you're right about her making the videos Thursday night. I think you're right that figuring out what dares she might have done might help us find her. You're still going to help me, right?" Tess asked, her face close to mine so she could see me in the dark.

I couldn't *not* help my sister, no matter how frightening

the situation was. And honestly, I couldn't not help Colette either. What if she was inside?

"Yeah." I sighed.

"Good," Tess said, nudging me with her shoulder.

I made a little sound that meant *Stop touching me*. We stopped in front of the house, looking up at the porch.

"I wonder if she's home." My eyes rose to the darkened main-floor windows, then to the second floor. "And I wonder what she does with all that space. It's huge."

Are you in there? I asked Colette with my mind. *Should we call the police? But . . . the Sea Witch was at the police station, so obviously they're already onto her. But what if they aren't, and you're trapped?*

I was so confused.

"We need to go up and look in the windows," I said, feeling seasick without even being on a boat.

"Are you serious?" Tess asked. We were gripping each other's arms so tightly that my hand was starting to fall asleep, but I didn't care.

"We have to at least check to see . . ." See what? I didn't know.

"Ohmygod," Tess chattered nervously. "Actually, maybe you're right: this might be the dumbest thing we've ever done. I seriously can't think of anything dumber right now. This is all Colette's fault. If she's not in trouble, I'm going to kill her."

A single porch light was on, hanging right above a big planter with a dead tree in it. The massive porch had nothing on it but a swing with no cushion; it was made of what looked like splintery wood.

"I don't see any clues, do you?" Tess whispered.

"No," I whispered back. "But I can't see much from down here. Maybe there's something in the planter. That's the only place to hide anything."

"I'm scared."

She would have been more scared had she known about the warning.

"It's only five steps," I said, picking up the bravery that Tess had somehow dropped. "We can do it." I pulled my arm from Tess's. "But I can't walk up steps linked like that." I shook my hand a little to get the feeling back. Then I shook it a lot when the pins and needles came.

I looked up at the windows again: they were all still dark.

"I don't think she's home," I said. "Let's look quick and get out of here." I took a deep breath and ran up the steps, like ripping off a Band-Aid.

"Ohmygod," Tess said behind me, then she climbed up, too.

I went straight to the planter and my heart leaped into my throat when I imagined a piece of taffy nestled inside the twisty branches of the dead tree. I jumped.

"What?" Tess whisper-shouted. She was right behind

me, and I really hoped she wasn't considering touching my shoulders. "Why did you jump?"

"I was excited! I thought I saw taffy in the planter. I thought Colette left it."

"Huh?" Tess whispered. "That's weird! Let's get out of here!"

"I'm just going to look to make sure . . . ," I said, peering into the dead branches one more time, to make sure I'd really imagined it. Suddenly there was a face in the long window next to the door, staring at me.

I screamed, then Tess saw her and screamed, and we both raced down the stairs. Like I was being pulled toward the ocean, I started running across the field-size lawn toward the bike path until Tess yelled that we had to get our bikes. Before I rounded the corner toward our bikes, I glanced back at the window.

The face was gone.

chapter 16

Fact: Most tornadoes happen
in the late afternoon.

IT WAS ALMOST ten o'clock—past typical tornado time and, honestly, past our bedtime—when Tess and I walked into the Sand Piper Diner, which was open until midnight on the weekends. I'd never been there that late before. Usually we went on special occasions, like when someone got a good grade on a test—well, when Tess did. I always ordered pumpkin pancakes with blueberries inside.

In the mornings, the patrons are usually regular families, tourist families, or nice older people (meaning not the Sea Witch). That night, there were three packs of rowdy high schoolers in the far corner and a few men who looked like logging truckers scattered around—plus an older couple who seemed to be fighting.

Colette smirked at us from the MISSING CHILD poster

taped to the wall near the cash register. I'd been in line behind her to have my school picture taken that day.

"Here, Frankie, you can use my brush," she'd said after running it through her bright red hair, making it as shiny as her lip gloss.

"Um, no," I'd said, frowning at the brush, thinking of lice and dandruff and other people's skin cells. Catching myself, I'd added, "I mean, no thank you."

Colette had looked hurt anyway.

"Can I use it?" Mia had asked from behind me. "I'm sure it won't make my hair look as good as yours . . ."

They'd smiled at each other, Colette with her freckle-face and Mia with her dimples, and I'd told myself inside that I was wrong for not being the kind of girl who wants to share brushes and lip gloss with her friends.

"It's late," I told Tess now. I looked away from Colette, feeling bad again. One of the high school boys was staring at us. "Maybe we should go home."

"We will," Tess said. "But let's eat first." She looked at me like Mom looks at me, like food will solve all my problems.

"I'm not hungry," I snapped . . . probably because I was hungry. Tess ignored me.

"Sit anywhere you like, girls," the waitress said, passing by the hostess stand with a tray full of food.

"Come on," Tess said, walking toward the booth farthest

away from the high schoolers. I followed Tess with my head down, shoulders forward, a frown on my face.

The waitress came over once she'd dropped off the food she'd been carrying, offering us menus.

"We'll have Tater Tots with ranch and two Cokes, please," Tess said.

"You got it," the waitress said, and she spun around and disappeared. I mean, she didn't literally vanish; she just walked into the kitchen. You're supposed to use metaphors when you tell stories: I don't know why, but people like them better than plain language. Whatever.

I swung my feet under the table and accidentally kicked Tess.

"Ouch," she said. "Will you please keep your feet on your side?"

I rolled my eyes at her but concentrated on not kicking her as I kept swinging my feet.

"What's wrong with you?" Tess whispered, leaning in. "Why are you in a bad mood all of a sudden?"

"I'm not!" I snapped. I was mad about being scared. I was mad that Colette's poster had reminded me of the type of girl I wanted to be—but wasn't. I was mad that we hadn't remembered anything about dare-or-scare. I was mad about Colette being missing and maybe hurt or dead. And, honestly, I was probably hungry. "I'm fine," I added.

"Fine?" Tess asked.

"Fine, I'll tell you, but don't freak out."

"Tell me what?" Tess asked, looking freaked out already.

"I ran into the Sea Witch at the police station earlier and she told me that kids who run around without their parents might get hurt," I blurted out.

Tess stared at me with big eyes. "She said they might get *hurt*?"

I nodded, thinking back. "Or maybe that you never know what will happen to them. Whatever, it was creepy. And she grabbed my wrist."

"Did she hurt you? Do you have a bruise?" Tess asked, looking down at my wrist.

"No, but . . ." Had the Sea Witch grabbed me hard, or just touched me? "That's not the point. The point is that Colette is probably in that crazy lady's house right now!"

The waitress brought the Cokes and Tess thanked her automatically. By the time I said a weak thank-you, she was too far away to hear.

"Maybe . . . ," Tess said about the possibility of Colette being at the Sea Witch's house. She looked confused as she took a sip of Coke. "Maybe we should call the police."

"But she was already *at* the police station!"

Tess nodded. I wished I hadn't told her because her reaction was too calm. And then she just changed the subject.

"We need to figure out what other dares Colette might have been doing—dares that all three of us did."

"No, we don't," I said through gulps of soda. "This is stupid. I can't remember the dares—and with the rest of the videos missing from Viewer, we're never going to remember. All we're doing is putting ourselves in scary situations. We're not going to find her! The police will have to!"

"Don't give up, Frankie," Tess said. "I still think you're right."

"So what?" I asked. "What does being right matter?"

"It matters if it helps find Colette," she said. "And it matters because . . ."

She stopped talking while the waitress set down our Tater Tots. I started eating like I'd never eaten before: I wasn't just hungry, I was starving. I held the Tater Tots with both hands like a squirrel.

"Because what?" I asked with food in my mouth.

"Because you deserve to be right sometimes," Tess said.

I scrunched up my eyebrows at her. I didn't know exactly what she meant, but I felt a lump in my throat that I was pretty sure wasn't a Tater Tot.

"Will you please tell me what happened?" Tess asked quietly. "Between you and Colette?"

The high schoolers erupted with shouts and laughter; one of them had spilled something. I didn't get why it was funny. They were smashed into three booths, but some were kneeling on the bench and turned backward so they could talk to two tables at once. They were leaning on everything, on the back of the booths, the windowsill, the tables. Leaning and laughing, looking so much older than us.

"I'm afraid to go to high school," I whispered, watching them.

"I think it's mostly the same as middle school," Tess whispered. I glanced at her and she was watching them, too, until two of the teenagers started kissing. Tess and I both looked away quickly, me making a grossed-out face and Tess blushing.

"Do you think that Colette has kissed Bryce?" I asked her.

"I know she has," Tess said. "She kissed him at the movies. And again, after school one time."

"Did she say she *liked* it?" I asked.

"I didn't ask her," Tess said. "But if she did it twice, she must have liked it the first time."

I looked back over at the kissing couple. They seemed like they were trying to eat each other's faces off, and the boy's hand was around the girl's body, resting on the lower part of her back. Like, way low. Like the top of her butt.

"Stop staring at them," Tess whispered.

"I'm not *staring*," I said, refocusing on my sister. "Would you let a boy try to eat your face off like that? In public?"

"No!" Tess said, making me feel relieved until she

added, "Not in *public*. But if a boy I liked wanted to kiss me, I'd let him." Her cheeks were bright pink, dotted with tiny freckles—not out-of-control freckles like Colette's, just faint dots the size of marks from a really sharp pencil under Tess's eyes and over the top of her nose.

"Do you like a boy?" I asked, concentrating on making sure my voice was low so I wouldn't embarrass her by letting anyone else hear.

"Sort of," she admitted. Now her mood-ring eyes looked closer to gold.

"Who?" I pressed in a whisper, leaning closer to her.

"Colin," she said, which made her cheeks turn a deeper shade of pink. She meant Bryce's best friend.

"Why do you like *him*?" I asked.

Tess frowned at me. "Why do you like Kai?" It was a whisper, so I knew she wasn't trying to embarrass me, but I still felt embarrassed.

How do you know that? I thought but didn't say, looking around the diner to make sure that no one was paying attention to us.

Tess must have realized I wasn't going to answer. She went back to her original question. "Will you *please* tell me what happened between you and Colette?"

"I don't want to talk about it," I said, angry that she was acting like she didn't remember. I noticed my heartbeat pounding, and the table felt so sticky I wanted to rush to the bathroom to wash my hands. Instead, I wiped them on my clothes.

"You promised you'd tell me," Tess said, tucking her hair behind her ear and looking at me with big eyes. The way she looked, like she had no clue in the world what I could be talking about, really irritated me.

"How can you pretend to be so innocent when you didn't stand up for your own sister?" I asked in a voice louder than I'd meant. Tess's cheeks turned pink again. She dipped her chin.

Instead of telling me to be quiet, though, she asked, "What are you talking about?"

"You just let them laugh at me. I *heard* you." I tried to keep my voice level because we were inside and there were people around. It was like holding on to Pirate's leash when she really, really wants to go in a certain direction.

Tess screwed up her face in confusion. I leaned in and hissed, "Stop acting like you don't know what I'm talking about! You were all in your room, studying for a test. It was you, Colette, Mia, and two other girls."

"Hold on," Tess said calmly, shifting in the booth. "Two other girls? Who?"

"How should I know?"

"We never study with anyone else!" Tess started biting her thumbnail, looking off in the distance like she was thinking really hard. Then she looked back at me quickly. "Do you mean Naomi?"

"Colette's weird neighbor?"

Tess nodded, smiling at me for calling Naomi weird. She really is. She's a close talker, which makes me uncomfortable, and she's always coming up with strange clubs like the "Blue Socks on Tuesdays" club. So yeah, Naomi's weird.

But I guess everyone is, in their own way.

"I have no idea," I said. "I don't know what her voice sounds like. It's not like I have any classes with her or anything."

"That has to be it," Tess said. "She's the only person who's ever come to a study group in my room except Mia and Colette. You know how Mom is about people in our rooms."

"Yeah," I said, never having run into that problem since I don't like people in my room, so I wouldn't ask to invite anyone. Or have anyone to invite anyway.

"Those are the only people who were there. You thought you heard someone else?"

I rolled my eyes, *really* not wanting to have this conversation. But you know how, when you don't want to talk about something, that's all the person you're with wants to talk about?

I grudgingly explained. "You were all studying and then someone asked about why I wasn't studying, and you said because I don't unless Mom makes me—which I do, by the way . . ."

Tess sighed and nodded.

" . . . and the other girl came in and then Colette started talking about how I take tests in a special room and—"

"What?" Tess interrupted, her eyebrows raised.

"And then everyone laughed because I like tornadoes and Mia called me a tornado brain and—"

"WHAT?!" Tess said loudly, not caring who heard her. A few of the high schoolers looked at us for a few seconds before they got bored and went back to their chatter.

"And I snuck away because I didn't want to hear you guys talk about me anymore."

Tess's hand flew to her mouth and her cheeks went red—but she looked mad instead of embarrassed this time. "That's what you've been upset about for, what, like two whole months?"

I nodded. "Wouldn't you be?"

"Of course!" she said. "I just wish you would have *told* me. That's a long time to have hurt feelings!"

"Why did I need to tell you? You were there!"

Tess inhaled and looked up at the ceiling of the diner, then exhaled loudly. "Frankie, do you honestly think that I wouldn't have said anything if I'd been there?"

"But I heard you," I said. "I heard you say that I only study when Mom makes me."

"Yes!" she said. "I said that when I was leaving to go get everyone sodas." She paused and took a big breath. "You thought someone else came *in*. But I went *out*."

"No, that's not what happened," I said, unsure. Or was it just not what I'd *thought* happened?

"Think about it, Frankie," Tess said. "Did you hear my voice after the thing about the studying? Did you hear me *say* anything else? Did you hear me *laugh* at you?" Her eyes welled up with tears. "You didn't! Because I never would!"

"Colette did," I said softly.

"Colette's not your sister. I am." She brushed away her tears as they fell. "I would never do that to you."

"But you're always mad at me," I said. "And you never want to do anything with me."

"You just stopped hanging out with us without any explanation and I thought . . ." She wiped her face again. "I thought you didn't want to do anything with *me*."

"Oh," I said, thinking about that.

The waitress came over. "You two need anything else?"

Tess asked for the check and the waitress pulled it from her apron and dropped it on the edge of the table. She left, and Tess picked up the check, curling the edges of it. She used to rip up paper or napkins or movie tickets or whatever was in her hands. I wondered if she was going to rip up the check.

"I'm so sorry," Tess said.

"It's okay," I said automatically, since that's what you say.

"No, it's not," Tess said. She set down the check and touched my hand across the sticky table. Despite it normally feeling awful to be touched, it felt okay to be touched by her—at least for a second. She must have sensed that because she took her hand away. "They were so rude. And it's one thing from Mia—you know, because you guys have never really been good friends—but from Colette it was . . ."

I nodded. The tears were there again without warning. I wiped my face with my sleeve.

"Let's go home," I said.

Tess didn't argue with me this time. "Okay, Frankie, let's go home."

chapter 17

Opinion: Some people believe that when you
dream about tornadoes, it's because you're
feeling out of control.

"I'M MAKING TEA," I told Tess when we arrived back at the
inn. We were ten minutes late for our eleven o'clock curfew;
we'd had to stop our bikes three times on the way home
from the diner to answer texts from Mom.

"I'm going to tell Mom we're home," Tess said, parking
her bike at the end of the line of loaners near the far wall
of the lobby. She leaned in and whispered, "And make up
something about the movie." She looked uneasy: Tess is a
rule-follower. "Do you want to come with me?"

I shook my head, shifting from one foot to the other. I
didn't want to go back outside where the April night had
turned cold. Inside, the fire was on, making the lobby toasty
warm. "I'm going to take my tea to my room."

No matter what time it is, there's coffee, tea, and

flavored water waiting for guests. Mom likes them to stay hydrated, I guess. Mint tea is something that sometimes helps me calm down, and we're never out of it.

"Okay, see you tomorrow," Tess said sadly. She hesitated at the side door, looking back over her shoulder at me like she wanted to say something. She didn't, though.

I filled a cup with steaming water and added a mint tea bag. I leaned against the wall, waiting for it to steep. I have to do the whole tea-making process down in the lobby because I don't like used tea bags in my room. I don't know why, it's just a thing.

While I waited, my brain played on high speed. I remembered the Sea Witch at the police station—maybe being questioned as a suspect! I thought of her telling me that kids running around without their parents could get in trouble; then, shivering, I thought about her face in the window at her house. I wanted to call Officer Rollins and tell him what she'd said to me. But what if she was really nice to the police and pretended not to know anything and they let her go? And what if she just went home to torture Colette? What if—

"Yo, did you or your sister use Lemonade?" Tyler, the overnight front desk attendant, interrupted my thoughts. He was pulling on his beard—*ick*—and tapping his pen on the counter in time to low music.

I looked at him blankly. "What are you talking about?"

"Lemonade is missing," he said, tugging his beard again. I wished he'd stop that. "Have you seen it?"

I looked at him like he was speaking German. "Huh? What's Lemonade?"

Tyler rolled his eyes at me and pointed over at the row of loaner bikes. "Haven't you ever noticed that they're all named after food? The ones you just brought back are Mint Chip and Black Licorice."

"No, they're not," I said.

But I went over to check. On the back wheel cover of the black bike, in swirly, cursive font, it said *Black Licorice*. Noticing now, I read down the row: the red bike was *Cherry Pie*, the orange was *Marmalade*, and the white one was *Marshmallow*.

"I always thought that was just decoration," I said.

Tyler sighed. "Now that you know it's not," he said, "have you seen Lemonade? The yellow one? No one signed it out."

"I know," I said. "I wanted to use it, but it's gone."

The steeping timer on my phone went off and startled me. Tyler shook his head and put on headphones, telling me that our conversation was over. I removed the tea bag, then added cream, which I like even though it looks kind of gross in the mint tea, and since my mom wasn't watching, I added sugar, too. I got a new spoon to stir everything, then went up to my room.

It was all too much to deal with that night. I vowed to

call the police in the morning and just let them decide what to do about the Sea Witch.

I took off my shoes and walked around piles of clothes and books to my bed. I took a sip of tea and set it on the nightstand, then flopped down, my head on the cool pillow. The window was still open; I listened to nature's sound machine outside. I wanted to check the TwisterLvr feed; I wondered if any tornadoes had happened today. But only for a few seconds, I think, because then I was asleep, somewhere else, a memory inside a dream.

I ran across the huge lawn in front of the Sea Witch's house, stomach muscles sore from laughing. I couldn't see anyone but knew I wasn't alone—I could hear a set of feet running behind me to the right and another to the left. The lawn gave way to longer beach grass: we pounded through, the tallest stalks tickling my palms, before reaching the path where three bikes were waiting for us.

"I'm doing the next dare!" I shouted, breathing heavily through a mischievous smile. "I'm going right now!"

"But it's getting dark!" a voice protested.

"It's dangerous," another agreed.

In my dream, their voices were different and their faces were blurry, but I knew they belonged to Tess and Colette. I just didn't know who was who. I hopped on the yellow bike: Lemonade.

"Wait! Frankie!"

"Don't go tonight!"

"This one is worth *all* of the taffy!" I shouted over my shoulder, curving around the bend in the path and dipping down out of sight. I couldn't see the ocean because of the bluff to my right, but I could hear it. The breeze blew my hair back and I was free to do anything. I could ride forever.

It wasn't quite dark yet, but the clouds made it look like the sun had gone to bed. I could still see the paved path well as it wove through the beach grass and squat little trees poking up here and there. I went by the benches that were put there in memory of someone. I went by the eagle-watching platform that Colette, Tess, and I used to use for a different dare.

"Jump off!" we'd challenge each other.

"Jump higher," we'd scream, and laugh.

In my dream, I rode Lemonade on the bike path until I reached Thirtieth. After a left and a quick right, I rode down Willows Road until it connected with North Head Road, then took another right. I pedaled my hardest, only pausing for breath in the parking lot at Beard's Hollow. I'd gone through Seaview and Ilwaco without noticing: the towns are so close together they're practically on top of each other. I continued up North Head Road because that would be the fastest way to the North Head Lighthouse—the end point of this amazing dare. I knew I'd be to my destination in about fifteen minutes because I'd done it before.

The first few blocks were flat, but then I was careful to stay to the far right on the hilly two-lane road: there wasn't a sidewalk and some parts plunged down to ditches or farther depths. Looking at the dense trees passing by as I pedaled my way up the hill, I swelled with pride. This was *my* dare. I would be the only one to do it!

In the way that dreams fast-forward, mine did, and next I was coasting downhill, where the roadside drops to a wooded ravine. With no cars in sight, I rode straight down the center line, taking my feet off the pedals and feeling like I was flying.

And then I was flying . . . on my bike, over the same route I'd ridden. And then I was back where I'd left my worrying sister and friend. But there was only one person waiting.

"You took Lemonade," she cried. I didn't know whether it was Tess or Colette. I couldn't place her voice and her face wouldn't hold still long enough to be in focus. "You took Lemonade."

"But I'm back now," I said. "Look, I'm back! I did the ultimate dare!"

She wasn't facing me, and it upset me, because I wanted her to be happy for me. And I wanted the other one, Tess or Colette, to be there, too, telling me I had done a good job.

"You took Lemonade," the girl said again.

"But I told you, I'm back!" I shouted at her.

And then her face was in focus—but it wasn't Tess's face. And it wasn't Colette's.

"You took Lemonade," I said to myself. "And you're not back. You're gone."

PART 3

The Rest

chapter 18

Fact: There have been instances of
tornadoes destroying lighthouses.

SUNDAY MORNING, THE real storm came.

Tess and I sat opposite each other at the kitchen table
in the cottage, each with a fleece blanket wrapped around
our shoulders because our PJs had gotten wet running over
from the inn. We were both holding mugs of tea that our
mom had made while we'd waited for the others. I had my
feet up on my chair and my mug rested on my knees, which
was keeping them from jittering. Pirate lay at the foot of
my chair.

The cottage was crowded.

Mom and Officer Rollins sat at the table with us;
Officer Saunders and a policewoman I didn't know sat on
the couch in the living room, which was really the same
room as the kitchen since there wasn't a wall separating

them; and Charles leaned against the kitchen counter with his arms folded across his chest, the orca tattoo on his arm facing out.

The recorder in the middle of the table had a green light illuminated on it. The clock on the microwave said 7:16 a.m. and we'd just finished telling the whole room about dare-or-scare.

It'd been two and a half days since anyone had seen Colette.

Officer Rollins tried to keep it all straight. "So you believe that Colette was making videos Thursday night, and something happened to her when she was filming—and that's why we can't find her?"

"Yes," Tess answered confidently.

"And you also believe that she changed the upload dates on the videos, so it would look like they were older than they are?"

"Yes." Tess nodded.

"Why?"

Tess looked at me, unsure. I shook my head. "We don't know," Tess answered for us.

"But you feel confident that she was re-creating your dare-or-scare game. Is that what you think, too, Frankie?" he asked me.

"I think so?" I said, feeling groggy and frazzled with

most of the police officers in Long Beach stuffed into the tiny cottage.

"And you initially suspected that Colette might be at Mrs. Sievich's residence?"

"Yes," I said, looking down at my hands, feeling stupid. Officer Rollins had already explained that the reason the Sea Witch had gone to the police station was that her property had been vandalized again—I guess it happened sometimes—and officers had gone there to check it out. So they were pretty sure Colette wasn't there. Maybe I felt a little sorry for the Sea Witch. I don't know.

It didn't matter anyway: the dream had made me remember where Colette was for sure—and she wasn't with the stuffed dead animals.

Rollins, as the other officers called him, rubbed his eyes and his forehead, just like he had on Friday. "Frankie, we've been looking for Colette for forty-eight hours straight. We're all exhausted. I don't want to hear that you think she *might* be out there. I need you to tell me *specifically* where you think she is."

Honestly, I thought I'd already said that, but maybe it was just the voice screaming in my head, telling them where to look. Or maybe I felt like I'd told the police because I'd told Tess about my dream, the dream when I remembered the best dare I'd ever come up with.

I took a deep breath, wondering: *What if I'm wrong?* But then I asked myself, *What if I'm right?*

"I think she was trying to do a dare I made up," I began. Everyone in the room was looking at me. Charles nodded, and my mom gave me a reassuring smile, but the way Tess held her chin high like she was holding mine up for me made me feel like it was all going to be all right. "It was around Halloween when I made it up. Tess and Colette had been to three haunted houses already and I knew if I chose to do a scare, they would come up with something terrible. So I had to make the dare really great."

"And?" Officer Rollins asked.

"I dared us to ride to the lighthouse."

My mom gasped.

Tess started biting her thumbnail and the officers in the living room took notes even though the recorder was on in the middle of the table, documenting everything I said.

"It's not that far," I said, turning my mug in my hands. "When I did it, it didn't even take me an hour."

I glanced at my mom, who did not look happy that I'd ridden by myself to the lighthouse. "Did you do it, too?" she whispered to Tess.

Tess looked at me guiltily, then back at Mom. "I told Frankie and Colette that I had, but I lied. I went halfway—but I got scared and turned around."

"I knew it," I muttered.

"Keep going, Frankie," Rollins said.

"Colette doesn't have a bike," I said. He looked at me like he didn't get what I was saying, so I added in explanation, "The yellow bike has been missing from our inn."

"Oh no," Mom murmured, understanding.

"She means that she thinks Colette took a bike from our inn to try the dare," Tess said.

"Yes," I said, nodding, keeping my eyes low.

"Frankie, when you called yesterday, you said there was a whole page of dares in your notebook," Rollins said. "Why would Colette choose this one?"

"I don't know," I admitted. "Tess thought maybe she picked dares that we all did—but Colette never did this one before. I wonder if she picked the hardest ones, or just the ones that were the least . . ."

"Least what?" Mom asked.

"Stupid?" I answered, thinking of the dare where you had to see how many marshmallows you could eat before you threw up.

"Maybe her goal is to do all of them," Tess said quietly. "Maybe she's not finished yet. Maybe she just . . ."

Tess stopped talking and everyone in the room went silent. I don't know why I felt guilty, but I did. Maybe because the dare had been my idea—and now we were sitting around talking with the police and Colette was missing, out there somewhere in the pouring rain.

Thunder rumbled the floor just to make me feel worse.

Officer Rollins looked worriedly out the window, then back at me. "To be clear, do you mean the North Head or Cape Disappointment Lighthouse?"

"Uh-huh," I said.

"Which one," he asked.

"North Head," Tess said.

"Okay, that's good, thank you, Tess," Officer Rollins said. To the other officers in the other room, he said, "That's, what, four miles?"

"More like five, maybe six," said Officer Saunders. He was sitting in my favorite seat on the couch; my thoughts were spinning too fast to care. I felt completely off the rails.

Officer Rollins turned back to me. "And what route did you use, Frankie, when you rode it?"

"Discovery Trail for part of it." I took a breath, knowing my mom wouldn't like the next part. "And North Head Road."

"The bike path?" Officer Rollins asked.

I shook my head no.

"Frankie!" my mom blurted out. "You could have been killed!"

Everyone got silent, probably thinking what I was: I could have been killed but hadn't been—but maybe Colette *had*. The policewoman was typing on her phone faster than a texting teenager.

"You mean Willows to North Head Road?" she asked, her eyes on her phone.

"I guess?" I asked back, because I don't pay attention to streets that much unless I have a reason to.

"Colette could have taken any of the north-south routes," Officer Rollins said to the other officers. "Call Martin from Ilwaco and see if they can spare anyone."

"We need to get the sheriff's office involved, too," the woman officer said.

"They already are," Officer Rollins said. He picked up the recorder and turned it off, then stood up. Seeming to fill the entire kitchen, he said, "We'll need to check around the roadways in both directions in case she reached the lighthouse and turned around—and Discovery Trail, too."

They moved toward the door, pulling their rain gear over their heads, their belts full of stuff, clanking and jangling. "Thank you, girls," Officer Rollins said before shutting the door to the cottage.

Tess hugged me.

I let her.

chapter 19

Fact: Tornadoes that happened before 1950 weren't reliably reported.

"HOW ARE YOU two?" Mom asked later, leaning up against the door frame, looking at us with concern. Tess and I were on the beds we'd slept in forever until we moved into the inn.

Mom went over and sat on Tess's bed. I felt jealous that she wasn't sitting on mine—but I didn't want her to sit on it either. I was confused by that feeling.

"We're fine," I said automatically.

"We're not fine," Tess said. "Did Officer Rollins call?"

Mom shook her head. "Not yet," she said. "I did speak with Colette's mother about an hour ago. The police are still searching. They're trying to move quickly but also be thorough."

"So they're going fast and slow at the same time?" I asked. "That makes no sense."

I looked up at the trio of paper hot-air balloons I'd made with a babysitter once hanging over my bed from hooks on the ceiling. The babysitter had told me to write something inspirational on them. In black marker, one said: *Something inspirational.* In purple marker, another said: *You can do it!* And in green marker, the one closest to me said: *We fly higher than lost balloons.*

"I don't know, Frankie," Mom said. "They're trying their best."

"Okay," I said.

"Do you want pancakes?" she asked us. "I have some blueberries to put in them."

"I want to go back to sleep," Tess said, rolling onto her side, facing the wall. "My eyes sting."

Mom started scratching her back. I was jealous of that, too, even though I can't stand it when she does it to me. It's like I craved and hated the idea of contact at the same time, which made me feel like an alien. Maybe I just wanted to feel like my mom loves me the same as she loves my sister.

"I'm going to the beach," I said, getting up from the too-small bed. I stepped into the rain boots I'd thrown near the bed, but something wasn't right.

"Ugh, I hate these socks!" I crashed down to the floor

and struggled to get the rain boots off so I could readjust my socks. Rain boots are the worst to get off. "Help me!" I shouted at my mom.

"How about some manners?" she asked, walking over to me. I stuck my foot in the air. She trapped my leg between her knees and yanked the left boot off. Then we went through the same process with the right. "Do you want to borrow a pair of my socks?" she asked softly as I grunted and growled at the pair I was wearing.

I was annoyed at her offer. I was annoyed about everything, and I didn't know how to not be.

Finally I got the sock seams lined up on both feet so that they didn't squish my pinkie toes when I put my feet back in the boots.

"There!" I said, standing up and putting my hands on my hips.

"Do you want me to come with you?" Mom asked.

"No," I said. Her face looked hurt, so I added, "I just want to be alone."

"Okay, Frankie, but don't go far—and take your phone. Just in case we hear anything."

I nodded and left the room. The cottage looked empty without all the people in it from earlier: it felt strange. I put on my raincoat over my pajamas, then took an apple from the fruit basket and my phone from the charger. It wasn't pouring anymore—just raining—but still I made sure my phone was deep in my pocket, protected from the water.

I would have taken Pirate with me, but she must have been somewhere with Charles. I missed her clanking tags as I trudged through the sand by myself, eyes on the solid light gray sky. I walked to the closest shelter, which only shelters you against wind, not rain, since it's open at the top.

I was surprised to find a familiar face already there.

"What are you doing here?" I asked.

"Why do you keep saying that to me?" Kai answered. He had a black hoodie up over his hair, which annoyed me because I liked seeing all the weird ways he styled it. I guess it *was* raining.

"I don't mean it in a mean way," I said, kicking the sand. "I'm surprised you're here is all."

"I'm meeting Dillon," he said, and I believed him because his skateboard was next to him, leaning against the bench with the wheels facing out. Also, he had on skate shoes. "We're going to do some tricks off the boardwalk. You can watch if you want."

"You're skating in the rain?" I asked.

"Rain or shine." Kai smiled, but it didn't seem like a real smile, just a polite one. "You should come."

"Thanks, but I'm not in the mood."

"Okay," he said, standing up. He looked at my outfit. "Are you wearing pajamas?"

"So?"

"Nothing," Kai said, stepping away. "Okaybye. Catch you later, Frankincense."

"What does that even mean?" I asked, rolling my eyes.

Kai shrugged. "Something to do with Christmas? You tell me. I'm Buddhist, yo."

"Okay, Mr. Buddhist, aren't you waiting for Dillon to get here?"

"You said you're not in the mood to talk." He pulled his hoodie strings tighter. I really wished he'd let his awesome hair free so I could see what it was doing today.

"No, I didn't. I said I'm not in the mood to watch skateboard tricks."

"Oh."

Kai came back and we both sat on the bench part of the shelter, with about a three-person space between us. Neither of us said anything until it felt so uncomfortable that I had to talk.

"The police were at our house this morning," I blurted out.

"No way," Kai said, his eyes wide, leaning forward on the bench. "Something to do with Colette? What happened?"

The whole story tumbled out of me easily—and with it came tears that I didn't really care about shedding in front of Kai. He didn't make a big deal of it either: he didn't say anything about it at all.

"I remember that dare," Kai said when I finished the part about the officers leaving to search the different paths to see if Colette had been doing the lighthouse dare and had an accident.

"You do?" I asked, surprised.

"Yeah, of course," Kai said. "Don't you remember? I shot the edit for you." I tilted my head sideways; he tried to remind me. "Yeah, your sister was at some camp and Colette was . . . I don't know where she was. But you wanted to do the dare on a certain day because it was sunny out and you were convinced that there was going to be a storm the next day." He laughed a little. "You told me that if no one was there to see it, then no one would believe it happened, and it would be like tornadoes that happened a long time ago but weren't recorded—so I made the edit as proof."

"You *did*?" I asked. "But in my dream, Tess and Colette were there."

"Frankfurter, dreams aren't real." Kai spun one of the wheels on his skateboard.

"Will you ever run out of weird names for me?" I asked, kind of liking the names even though they were so cringey.

Kai shrugged, smiling. He didn't answer me. Instead, he said, "I can't believe you spaced that I was there."

"Yeah, I know," I said.

I thought back for a long time and finally there Kai was, at the blurry edge of my memory, not getting mad when I yelled at him to move out of the way or get closer or hold still. Telling Dillon he was too busy to skate that day. Standing with me in the sun and the rain.

I didn't want to tell him I remembered because I felt like he might think I was lying. Instead, I asked, "Why didn't you ever do the dares with us—or the scares even?"

He smiled, but it seemed like it had some sad in it. "Duh, you guys never asked me to."

Kai looked off in the distance and waved. I turned and saw Dillon standing by the ramp to the boardwalk from the beach. Kai stood and picked up his skateboard. Looking at me, he said, "I always liked helping you, though. It was fun."

He gave a little wave and walked over to where Dillon was standing. I saw him say something to Dillon, then Dillon looked my way. I pulled my feet up under my knees on the bench, wondering if I should go watch them do tricks. But they jumped on their skateboards and took off down the boardwalk while I was weighing the pros and cons. That happens to me a lot: I consider something too long and miss the thing I was considering.

I felt bad.

I felt bad because I did actually want to watch the tricks.

I felt bad because Kai was gone.

I felt bad because I'd never asked him to do a dare.

I felt bad because I'd never noticed that he'd wanted to.

———

FROM THE SHELTER, I saw a police car pull into the parking lot of the inn. I watched two people shapes walk toward the cottage and my heart felt like it was going to break through my rib cage. I ran my fastest back home. I was sure that they'd found Colette—but I didn't know whether they'd found her alive or dead—and my brain was an EF5 tornado.

As I ran, I thought at her:

Why did you go alone?

Did you know you were going to go when you came to my room?

Would you have asked me for help if I hadn't yelled at you?

Why did I ever make up that dare?

It's not my fault.

Why are you so bad at riding a bike?!

Maybe it is my fault.

It's not my fault!

"It's not my fault!!!" I shouted into the wind.

I wondered if anyone heard me.

chapter 20

Fact: The damage path of a tornado
can be more than one mile wide.

TESS WAS SOBBING, folded over, face in a throw pillow on the couch. I couldn't remember the last time Tess had cried like that; I stared at her with my mouth open for a few seconds. I felt like my head was disconnected from my body. I looked down at my muddy feet and struggled out of my boots, getting them to actually come off when I stepped on the heels, thinking that my mom wouldn't want me to track stuff inside. It was a weird thing to be thinking about, but I was in a daze.

I knew Colette must be hurt—or worse. Then I thought of the only time I'd ever seen her hurt before.

It was last year, and we'd walked all the way down the beach to the rocky cove one Sunday afternoon. In some ways, the cove is the best place on the beach because it's sheltered from the wind—so it's nice year-round. Steep black rocks with a forest on top jut up to form a wall that wraps around the sand. Smaller, sharp rocks with barnacles stuck to every surface are either right at the edge of the water, or swimming in it, depending on the tide. The way that the cove was formed, the waves come in from two directions at once, fighting with each other, angry and beautiful. Huge spray kicks up when the fighting waves clash, seagulls watching and snacking on the barnacles like Cheerios.

"My parents keep getting in fights," Colette said, looking out toward the waves. Her red hair was pulled back in a high ponytail and she had on a blue plaid shirt I'd always liked. "I'm afraid they're going to get divorced."

"That sucks," I said, not knowing what else to say.

"Yeah. My mom wants to move."

"No!" I shouted. "You can't!" I thought of how I'd be alone if Colette moved. How I'd have no one to come to the cove with. I thought of myself.

"I know," Colette said. "I'd die."

I started up a pile of barnacle-covered rocks. They weren't steep, but they were jagged. Colette followed me in her flip-flops. When we were at the top, we watched the ocean fight without saying anything.

"Maybe you can live here with us if your parents move," I told her. "You're twelve, you should be able to have a say in where you live."

"My parents don't think so," Colette said.

"You can't leave," I said, feeling desperate.

We'd both been so distracted by the topic that neither of us was paying attention to the water, and soon we were on a tiny island for two. The tide had risen to the point where, if we were to jump off right then, we'd be in water up to our chests—and would potentially be sucked out to sea or battered against the rocks.

"Crap!" Colette shouted, instantly panicking. "We're going to be stuck out here and drown!"

"Calm down," I said, rational. "We just have to wait for the waves to flow out again and jump down. Our feet might get a little wet, but we'll be fine."

She started crying, which shocked me.

I felt brave and ready to handle the situation, which sort of shocked me and sort of didn't. That happens to me sometimes. Sometimes I'm invincible.

"It's going to be okay," I said to her, edging to the side of the rocks. "See? Look, it's already starting to pull back." The water was quickly retreating. "Get ready to jump down to the sand."

"I'm scared," Colette said. I looked around to see if there were any adults just in case we needed help. Two fishermen were on another cluster of rocks. I waved at them, one waved back, and I hoped that reassured Colette that they'd probably help if we called out.

"Come on, jump now!" I jumped, my heels digging deep into the sand when I landed. Colette froze, then a few seconds later took two steps toward the edge. Except one of her flip-flops snagged on the rock. She fell more than jumped off, landing on her hands and knees in the sand and lurching forward so her head hit the next boulder over. Barnacle-covered boulders are sharp.

I reached down and grabbed her hand to help her up. With only one flip-flop and a bleeding forehead, she managed to run behind me to dry sand, chased by the surf the whole way.

When we were safe, we looked at each other and exploded into laughter. One of the fishermen had been keeping an eye on us. He shook his head and turned back toward the water.

"That was awesome," I said.

"No, it wasn't!" Colette said, but she was smiling, so I thought she thought it was awesome, too. People don't always say what they mean.

My mom's voice brought me back to the present. "Frankie?" she asked. "Are you listening?"

The policewoman from earlier was back.

"Is Colette dead?" I asked loudly.

"She's hurt but she's alive," Mom said quickly. She rushed over and put her arm around me. I let her keep it there for a few seconds, then stepped away.

"She's not okay, is she?" I asked, looking at the officer, then at my mom.

"Frankie, I said she's alive," Mom answered. "That's a good thing. She's hurt, yes, but she's alive, thank goodness. I'm going to call her parents and see what they need."

"It's probably best to give them a few hours—" the officer started to say to my mom before I interrupted.

"Where was she?" I asked.

"About a mile from the lighthouse," the officer answered.

Just a mile—a mile is nothing . . . unless it's the width of a tornado. But a mile on a bike is easy.

"Did she finish the dare?" I asked, my voice sounding higher than normal, eyes bouncing back and forth between my mom and the officer.

"Frankie, I hardly think that's relevant right now when—" Mom began.

"Did she finish the dare or not?" I shouted, balling my fists at my side. *Just tell me if she finished the dare or not! I screamed in my brain. Tell me if she finished, because if she did, she would have been riding on the more dangerous side of the road—the side with the drop-off into a ravine. She'd be in worse condition if she had finished!* I thought I was screaming out loud, so they'd all understand that I was talking about Colette's health, not some dumb game. But my heart was racing, and my thoughts were spinning. I felt like a human tornado. Some words came out, but some stayed in my head. "Tell me if she finished! Just tell me!"

Tess rose from her place on the couch and wiped her eyes. She looked at me, confused.

"Frankie, the game doesn't matter anymore," she said, probably trying to help. It didn't.

"I don't care about the game!" I shouted.

"Then why do you keep asking if she finished the dare?" Mom asked.

"Ugh!" I shouted at her before stomping my feet several times. Right then, Charles and Pirate came in. Charles looked around the room.

"I saw the police car when we came back from our walk," he said, his face twisted in concern. "What's going on?"

I was still stomping.

"I'll tell you in a minute," Mom said to Charles. "We have a situation here." Then, to me, "Stop that!"

She looked flushed and embarrassed. I desperately wanted to suck it all back in, inside my skin, all the anger and miscommunication and tears. I wanted to vacuum it back up into the sky, like when a tornado changes its mind and returns to the funnel cloud. But it'd already touched down.

"Frankie—" the woman officer began.

I cut her off. "TELL ME IF COLETTE FINISHED THE

DARE!" I screamed at the top of my lungs. "THAT'S ALL I'M ASKING!"

"Whoa," Charles said, holding up his palms. "We need to—"

"Go to your room!" my mom shouted back at me. "You are not allowed to scream at a police officer!"

"But she's allowed to treat me like a baby and not tell me what happened?" I shouted, backing toward the door.

Everyone was standing up now. I thought that the policewoman should have been angry, but instead, she looked like she pitied me, which made it worse.

"Frankie, maybe you just need a second to breathe," Charles said. His eyes had tears in them. "Maybe—"

"Maybe if the police knew how to do their jobs, then Colette wouldn't be hurt right now!" I yelled. "Maybe if they'd found her faster, everything would be okay!"

This made the officer purse her lips, but she didn't say anything.

"I'm so sorry," my mom said. "She tends to get emotion—"

That's all I heard before I slammed the door, leaving without bothering to step back into my boots. I screamed the loudest I could outside, a high-pitched horrible scream that felt like it would break my own eardrums. There was a family walking by and all four of them looked at me, startled.

"Stop looking at me!" I yelled.

The mom took hold of the youngest kid's hand and they all rushed away. I was acting like the type of person who scared little kids, and I couldn't begin to control it.

The wet pebbles and puddles under my socks prevented me from stomping as much as I wanted to, so I screamed again, then leaned over and picked up a rock, throwing it in the direction of the water. It landed with a *thud* in the tall beach grass. The release of the rock had felt good: it'd felt productive. I picked up another rock, this one the size of a golf ball. I cocked my arm back and threw it hard. It thudded louder to the earth. I threw five more rocks of about the same size, each throw more forceful than the last. My shoulder felt like it was going to rip out of the socket, but I was starting to feel a little better.

I saw a spectacular rock near the entryway to the inn: a polished gray rock the size of a large potato. It was much heavier when I picked it up and I knew it'd make the best thud yet. I stepped back so I was close to the building: I would need a running start. My socks were completely soaked, slapping the ground as I walked. I pulled my arm back over my right shoulder, rock in hand, ready to hurl it and all my anger away. But I guess I was *too* close to the building. I was too close, specifically, to the huge pane of glass that my mom calls a "picture window" and that looks to the west from the lobby.

The tip of the rock hit the glass when I pulled my arm back.

The world stood still for a few seconds. Then I heard what sounded like ice popping when lukewarm soda is poured over it. The first shards broke free and huge sheets of glass followed, crashing to the ground around me. Before I knew it, I was an island in a sea of broken glass.

"Mom!" I screamed in a different way, a terrified way. "Help me!" I held my arms close to my body and didn't move. There were tiny pieces of glass all over my pajamas and my socks. "Help, come quick!"

The door to the cottage flew open and my mom came running out with Tess, Charles, and the police officers behind her. When my mom saw the glass, she paused and gasped. I knew she was going to be madder than she'd ever been: I'd probably be grounded for a year. But at first, she didn't look mad: she looked terrified.

She started running again, stopping at the edge of the scene.

"Are you hurt?" she asked. She looked at my shoeless feet, then her eyes moved up to inspect me.

"I don't think so," I said.

"Don't move," she said to me, looking around for something. "I need . . ."

I held still as stone.

"Let me get her," the policewoman said. "I'll carry her over the—"

"I've got it," Charles said, taking a step onto the glass. I think he was going to try to pick me up.

"No," my mom said, grabbing his arm. "She can't . . . you know she doesn't like being touched . . . you'll just make it worse."

Charles winced, probably knowing she was right. It's true that I'd never hugged him and that I shied away from the kind of play fighting he did with Tess, but not because I don't love him or anything. I thought he knew that, but it sure didn't look like he did right then. He looked crushed.

Mom glanced around again, then seemed to decide. She took a step onto the pile of glass herself, and it crunched like tortilla chips under her shoe. She took another step, and another, and another. Then she was in front of me. "Get on my back."

I couldn't jump up for fear I'd miss and slide back down onto a nest of broken glass. My mom bent low and, not wanting it to cut her, I gently shook as much of the glass as I could from my clothes before wrapping my arms tightly around her neck. I practically strangled her when she stood up again with me holding on. I wrapped my legs around her hips and she crunched us both out of the glass.

I started shaking right after she set me down. Now,

apparently, I was a person who vandalized businesses. I started crying again, because I didn't want to be that person. I cried because I was confused by who I was.

"I'm sorry," I whispered to my mom. She'd moved away. She was standing over by the glass debris again in the rain, her hands on her head, staring at the hole that'd been a window. When she looked back at me, covering her mouth, she had tears streaming down her cheeks.

She hadn't heard me apologize.

chapter 21

Fact: The severity of comas is classified on a
number scale, just like tornadoes.

"DID YOU KNOW that according to the Glasgow Coma Scale,
a person with a score of only three or four after twenty-four
hours will most likely die?" I asked.

"No, I didn't know that," Gabe said. "Thanks for telling
me."

It was Monday, the day after the police had found
Colette. Other kids were in school, but Mom hadn't made
me or Tess go—except she *had* made me come to see Gabe.
Gabe and I were in his office over the business that's a tan-
ning salon, a knitting shop, and a coffeehouse in one. I was
sitting in the comfy red chair that Gabe usually sat in, but
I didn't like it very much. Gabe wouldn't let me sit in my
normal spot on the couch—either he wanted to mix things
up to see if I'd freak out about the changes or he just felt like

sitting on the couch. Instead of being mad about it, I tried to focus on my newfound knowledge about comas.

"A person with a score of more than eleven will most likely live," I said. "I don't know what Colette's score is."

I was drawing tornadoes on a notepad, not making eye contact with Gabe.

"You seem to know a lot about comas," Gabe observed.

"Uh-huh," I answered. "A person somewhere in the middle has about a fifty-fifty chance of recov—"

"Frankie," Gabe interrupted.

"What?" I looked at him. He pushed up his black-framed glasses, which weren't as good as his other ones.

"We're running out of time today, and I want to be sure that we're able to talk about you—not just comas," Gabe said. I really didn't like that he'd switched glasses.

"I don't want to talk about me," I said. "I'm fine." I waited a second, biting my tongue, trying not to say what I was thinking. But with everything that'd happened, I couldn't hold things back very well. "I don't like those glasses: they look too . . . blocky. Your blue glasses are better."

"Hmm," Gabe said, leaning forward to take a sip of tea. I liked that he always made me tea and didn't care if I doodled while we talked. "How does Colette being in the hospital make you feel?"

"That's a stupid question," I said, making a big X through

the last tornado I'd drawn. I glanced up at Gabe to see if his neutral expression had changed when I'd said *stupid*.

"I'm sorry you feel that way," Gabe said, twisting his wedding ring, face still neutral. "Hey, will you make me a deal?"

"Maybe," I said.

"I know you don't want to start taking medication again," Gabe began. I grunted. "But I don't think you're being honest about how you're feeling—and if you're not being honest, then it's harder for me to figure out how to help you."

"Is that a threat?" I asked, my pen scratching around and around on the page.

"Wow, Frankie," Gabe said. "No, it's absolutely not a threat. I'm saying that I understand that you want to make the choice not to take medication—and if that's your choice, then I'm here to help you. But you need to do some work, too. I want you to agree to come here twice a week and do a worksheet in between. You can't blow off our appointments anymore. And you need to try to talk to me about what's happened with Colette. Do you think you can do that?" I shrugged, my eyes on the paper. "Frankie, will you please look at me?"

I looked up at him. Behind the awful glasses, his dark eyes were kind, as usual. Gabe is hard to be mad at or disagree with. Do you know adults who aren't like other adults,

241

who just get you more than normal grown-ups? Gabe is one of those.

"What?" I asked.

"Colette's Glasgow Coma Scale score is a five," he said.

"How do you know?"

"Because I know her doctor," he said.

"You're probably not supposed to tell me that," I said. I scratched my head: it itched even though I'd taken a shower that morning.

"Definitely not," Gabe said, "but I know you do better with facts. I know surprises are very challenging for you. This," he said, "is not a surprise you need to have."

"So you're saying she's going to die." I swallowed hard and looked back down at the paper filled with tiny, medium, and huge tornadoes. There were more tornadoes than white space.

The wind blew through the open window and rustled some papers on Gabe's desk. We sat in silence for seventeen ticks of the noisy clock. I pushed my bangs out of my eyes: they were too long.

Colette was going to die, probably.

I stood up because my mom would be here to pick me up any minute. "Bye, Gabe. I'll see you on Thursday."

chapter 22

Myth: People always wake from
comas instantaneously like on TV.

"ARE YOU AWAKE?" Tess asked from her room the next morning. The sun was barely up but I'd been awake awhile.

"Yeah," I said, feeling trapped. I'd slept with my weighted blanket the night before. It'd been comforting at bedtime, but now it was crushing me. I was sweaty, and I struggled as I kicked it off, the superheavy blanket landing on the floor with a *thud*. "Are you?"

"No," she said. No one laughed.

Our connecting doors were open, so I could hear her easily. I pictured her lying halfway off her bed with her hair all crazy.

"Are you going to school?" I asked. Mom had said we didn't have to—that we could take the whole week off if we wanted. It wasn't as great an offer as you might think since no matter where we were, it wouldn't change Colette's situation.

"I'm going," Tess said. "And I have to leave soon, or I'll be late for zero period. We're sculpting today." It didn't sound like she was moving. "Are you?"

"I think so," I said, feeling like school might be better than home. I had an extra hour to think about it since my day wouldn't start until first period.

From my bed, I listened to Tess shuffle around her room, getting ready. She told me goodbye and left, and I finally got up, getting tangled in the weighted blanket on the floor and tripping.

"Stupid blanket!" I said, growling at it.

I ate the only cereal I like in the world with milk from the mini-fridge in my room. I didn't need a jacket because it looked warm outside. I left my room but turned around because I'd forgotten my backpack. I left again, then turned around because I'd forgotten a snack and my mom says I have to take one every day or I'll get hangry.

In the lobby, I asked Charles if I could ride Black Licorice and he said it was okay. I walked the bike outside and put on my helmet while Pirate followed, wagging her tail. When I kicked off and started coasting through the parking lot, Pirate ran next to me, her tags clanking happily. She stopped at the edge of the lot and barked: *goodbye!*

"Have a good day, Pi!" I called over my shoulder.

I rode by the horse corral, the new mini-golf course, and the go-kart track, thinking of Colette, wondering whether she'd be able to do those things again. No one really knew what had happened to her because she hadn't been awake yet to tell them, but Tess thought Colette had been trying to apologize to me by starting up the dare-or-scare game again. Tess thought that Colette had thought that the game was really the only way to show me that she was sorry— because to Colette, dare-or-scare had always been our special thing, just the three of us.

I didn't know what to think about all of that, but I knew about her Glasgow Coma Scale score, which meant that I knew I'd probably never find out what Colette's intentions had been.

I hadn't told Tess about the score, though.

At school, I left Black Licorice in the bike rack without a lock. I stopped by my locker to get a notebook and went to homeroom, feeling the walls as I walked through the school. In my classroom, I sat at my own private desk island by the window and checked the online feed of a brain-injury survivor while the class filled up.

"What's that?" a familiar voice asked over my shoulder.

I angled the screen so that Kai could see it. While he looked at my screen, I checked out his shoes: they were black suede with dark brown accents.

"This girl was in a car accident and the doctors put her

in a coma so that her brain wouldn't swell up." I refocused on my phone and tapped the screen to enlarge a picture of the girl in the hospital: her face was bruised, one eye was swollen shut, and her head was wrapped in gauze. "Now look at her, though." I opened another picture: of the girl in a soccer uniform. "She had to relearn how to talk and walk, but now she can play sports and stuff again."

"Cool," Kai said. His hair was in his face today; he pushed it back and it fell right into his eyes again. "I hope that's how it'll be for Colette."

"Me too," I said.

"My mom said they tried giving Colette hypothermia to try to make her wake up." Kai stepped away from me a little, which I appreciated.

"They froze her?" I asked. "That's terrible."

He made a face. "I know, it sounds like torture. But I guess it can help coma patients wake up or something."

I looked down at my phone screen again. "Colette's not like this girl. Colette went into a coma all by herself. The doctors didn't put her in one."

"Is that better or worse?"

"How should I know?"

Someone hit Kai on the shoulder with a wadded-up piece of paper and he turned around to see who it was. When he saw Dillon laughing across the room, he bent over and threw it back at him.

The bell rang.

"See ya, Frankarama."

Kai smiled a sweet, sad smile at me and went over to his desk in the normal part of the classroom. I still had a desk over there, too, if I wanted it. I just liked the desk island for now.

"Take your seats, please," Ms. Garrett said. "Marcus! It's time to settle down. Everyone, put your phones away and quiet down—that means you too, Tess and Mia. We may only have six weeks left of school, but there's still learning to do."

Six whole weeks left of school: I couldn't believe it was still April. So much had happened since the last time I was in this classroom just four days ago, it felt dizzying.

Like she felt the same way, Tess looked over and held up her hand, a weak high five, or a wave without any movement. Her shoulders were more bent forward than usual, and she looked fragile, like she might break. I waved back, an actual wave, and she smiled, but barely. I wondered if she wished she were at home. I wondered if I did.

Tess looked down at her desk, her dark hair covering her face.

I did my math homework in fifteen minutes because it was totally easy, then got out *Call of the Wild*, hoping to finish reading it before the period ended. I still had to finish a paper on it—I had to *start* a paper on it, actually. But then the phone rang on Ms. Garrett's desk. Everyone looked up at her while she talked to whoever was on the other end.

After she hung up, she looked at *me*.

"Frankie, Principal Golden would like to see you."

"Why?" I asked.

"She didn't say," Ms. Garrett said, pursing her lips and making her face look even more birdlike.

A bunch of kids made noises like *oooh* and *waaaa* and *uh-uhhh*. Some laughed. One—Kai—just looked at me with a worried expression like the one that was probably on my face right then, too.

I hadn't told Kai about the coma scale score either.

"And you too, Tess."

The other kids didn't make any sounds when Tess's name was called.

I left my stuff and took a hall pass from Ms. Garrett. In the hallway, I realized Tess had brought her bag with her. I went back in and got my stuff, causing everyone to turn and stare at me. I wanted to shout at them to leave me alone. But then I noticed Kai's warm smile and it made me feel calmer.

"What do you think is going on?" I asked Tess, back in the hallway.

"It must be something about Colette," she said. "Otherwise why would they call us both?"

We started walking toward the front office, our footsteps in sync. I wondered if Tess noticed, but didn't ask her because I thought she'd think it was weird that I had. Maybe she wouldn't have. I don't know.

"It has to be about Colette, right?" Tess asked. She bit her pointer fingernail.

"Unless Mom or Charles died or something."

"Ohmygod, Frankie! That's an awful thing to say."

"Okay," I said, wishing I knew as well as Tess did which things would be considered awful—*before* I said them. Frustrated, I thought of some advice Gabe had given me— that people understand you better if you actually talk to them—and so I shared what I was thinking as we passed the classrooms in the English hall. "It's not like I *want* to say awful things, you know."

"I know," Tess said.

"I just say the truth, mostly."

"I know."

"But a lot of people consider the truth to be an awful thing," I said, scrunching up my eyebrows. "Am I supposed to lie? Maybe I'm just bad at lying."

"You're not supposed to *lie* to people," Tess said. "But you're not supposed to say every bit of truth that you think, because some of it is harsh. It comes out as being rude—or insensitive."

I knew all of this from therapy, but it was different hearing it from my sister.

"I don't want to be rude or insensitive."

"Frankie, you're not," she said. I looked down at my shoes. "You're *not*," she said again. "You have a really big heart. And you have a lot of great ideas in your head. But sometimes you just don't have a filter."

"So what's in my big heart and head falls out of my mouth?" I asked, smiling, sort of joking and sort of serious.

Tess smiled back, nodding. "Yeah."

We were outside the main office; Tess stopped, an anxious look on her face. "You know, it makes you who you are, though, and that's good."

I looked away, feeling awkward.

"I'm serious, Frankie," Tess said, touching me on the arm, then taking her hand away quickly. I touched my other arm to balance myself out. "Because you don't have a filter, you spoke up about what you thought had happened to Colette. You spoke up, and it's the reason they found her. She might still be missing right now if you had a filter."

She might be dead anyway, I thought. *Maybe that's why we're being called to see the principal.*

I just thought it, though, because saying it probably would have upset Tess. See? I have a filter . . . sometimes. Maybe it just needs to be changed more than other people's.

IF YOU'VE ONLY seen a hospital on TV, I'm going to be honest with you and tell you that TV is a liar.

The reason Tess and I were called to the office was because Colette's parents were getting desperate and they wanted us to go and try to talk to Colette to see if it'd get a reaction out of her. I guess freezing Colette hadn't worked— I mean, why would it?—and now they wanted to see if hearing familiar voices would help.

"I wonder why they didn't ask Mia to come," I asked Tess as we walked through the hospital doors behind our mom. The doors had slid open automatically, and I wanted to go back out and try it again, but I kept moving. "It smells in here. Gross." I plugged my nose.

"Shh," Tess said. Her face was pale and she looked like she might throw up.

"It's not a library," I said. "The point of us coming here is to talk. I wonder if it will work. And, really, why isn't Mia here? Is she coming, too?"

"I don't know," Tess whispered. "Maybe they didn't ask her because she and Colette haven't been friends for as long."

"So?" I asked.

"So she'd know our voices better," Tess said, looking

around warily. There was an old woman by herself in a wheelchair and she was crying. I looked away.

"That's logical," I said.

Our mom stopped at the information desk and asked which way the ICU was. That stands for "intensive care unit," and I was about to find out that it's exactly where you don't want to be in a hospital.

We went in the direction the information-desk woman had said, down the hall to the left and to the elevator bank at the end. Inside the elevator, Mom pressed the button for floor three and I stared up at the ceiling.

"An elevator would be a terrible place to be in a tornado," I said. "Or in any natural disaster, really."

The elevator doors opened, and it smelled even worse on this floor: like cleaning solution, mashed potatoes, and sickness. "Gross," I said again.

"Frankie, please keep your voice down," Mom said. "People are trying to rest and get well."

I had to try really hard not to point out, again, that a hospital wasn't a library and we'd been specifically asked to come here to talk. I didn't think that I should argue with my mom, though. We walked down the shiny floor to a nurses' station; my mom asked where Colette was. The nurse pointed to wide double doors with push bars in the middle. I followed Mom and Tess through to the ICU.

The room was about half the size of our gymnasium at

school, dim because the windows were all covered, divided into small sections by blue curtains on rods with wheels: movable fabric walls. Each small section had a bed in it. I couldn't see everyone, but I stopped and gaped for a few seconds at the patients lying in the beds I could see until my mom grabbed me by the wrist.

"Don't do that," I said, pulling my wrist away, then wrapping my fingers around my other wrist to even myself out. I followed my mom.

"Please remember to be kind," she whispered.

"I am," I insisted. *Do you think I'm a mean person?* I wondered but didn't ask her. We were rounding a fabric wall and there, in a twin bed on wheels with guardrails on the sides, was Colette. "Yikes," I breathed.

Tess spun around and slumped down so she could slam her face into Mom's shoulder; Mom hugged her tight.

"I know it's heartbreaking to see her like this," Colette's mom said, standing up from one of two chairs against what would have been a wall, if the wall wasn't a blue curtain. Colette got her red hair from her mom, but Colette's mom had a short cut with some gray in it. "Thank you both for coming. We appreciate it so much, and also you helping the police like you did."

"Uh-huh," I said in response, my eyes on Colette, wishing I wasn't looking at what I was looking at. My mom and Colette's mom worked on comforting Tess while I stared.

There were so many weird and terrifying things about the situation. I dug my thumbnails into my pointer, middle, ring, and pinkie fingers, over and over, while I looked.

First, Colette had her eyes closed. You might say, *duh*, but it's not like I'd ever stared at her while she was asleep before. She looked completely different. Open, her eyes would have given me clues about what she was thinking or saying, but closed, they said nothing. I did not like Colette's closed eyes at all.

Pointer, middle, ring, pinkie.

Poke, poke, poke, poke.

Second, there was a tube in her mouth and the outside of it was taped to her cheek—and the tape or the tube or both were pulling the right side of her mouth over in a way that made her look just flat-out creepy.

The others were talking in a whispered huddle. Tess was asking questions I probably wanted to know the answers to, but I didn't try to join their conversation. I went on with my list of horrors.

Third, there was a pole attached to a bag attached to a tube attached to a needle—attached to her arm. That's all I'm going to say about that.

Fourth, the beeping. I like music and the loud noises of crowds don't bug me. But if I'm in a quiet place and there's a noise that cuts through the quiet—something unexpected that's not supposed to be there—it can drive me to the point of screaming.

Beep. Beep. Beep. Beep. Beep.

Stop it, stop it, stop it!

If it stops, she'll be dead. It's monitoring her aliveness.

Beep. Beep. Beep. Beep. Beep.

My annoyance grew and grew, and turned into something that felt more like anger at the beeps. My heartbeat quickened, and my head got hot. I balled my fists and knocked my knuckles against my thighs, purposely out of time with the beeping.

The others were still talking, ignoring me. I knew I couldn't scream in the hospital: I didn't need my mom to tell me that. But I didn't know what to do. Taking a deep breath only sometimes works, but I couldn't do that even if I'd wanted to because I would have been breathing in that *smell*. I searched my brain for other strategies Gabe had taught me. *What was that one? Oh right: Think of a list of things that start with the same letter.* I chose the letter C for Colette. *Camel, car, candy* . . . Each one appeared in my mind at the same beat as the beeps. It was so annoying!

What do I do?

Beep.

I want to leave!

Beep!

Why did you run off and do this to yourself? I screamed at Colette in my mind.

Beeep!!!

And right then, I remembered something.

We were in third grade, I think. There was a school play, *The Three Little Pigs*. I played the role of a lamb and Tess and Colette were both pigs. I'd desperately wanted to be the other pig.

"It's not fair!" I'd cried when I saw the assigned roles posted in the hall. "I don't want to be a lamb! I knew all my lines and I should be a pig!"

"Sorry, Frankie," Tess said. "I wish you were the other pig, too."

Tears shot out of my eyes like sprinklers and I kicked the wall underneath the poster. I kicked it again harder and grunted. Tess's face turned red and she looked around to see who else was watching.

"You're going to get in trouble," Colette warned. "Stop kicking the wall."

I kicked it again, even harder this time. It hurt my toes, but I didn't care. I wailed loudly in the hallway. A teacher would probably come out soon and tell me to go to the principal, and then I'd probably have to work on art and talk about how outbursts at school aren't okay. I didn't want any of those things to happen, but my body did its own thing.

I kicked the wall yet another time.

"Frankie!" Colette said. "Here, look at me." I didn't at first. I couldn't see through my anger.

"Frankie, please!" Tess said, clearly so embarrassed. "You have to stop. Just pay attention to Colette."

"Come on," Colette said. "Look, do this." She dropped her backpack on the floor and was standing with her hands out, palms turned up.

She looked so strange I forgot to be mad for a second. "Are you praying?" I asked. "You look really weird."

Colette laughed. "It kinda looks like it," she said. "But no, I'm turning my palms up. You should try it. When I'm upset, it always makes me feel better."

"It looks stupid," I said.

"Maybe, but it makes me feel better when the air hits my palms," Colette said. "My mom told me to do it. She says it makes you feel more open to possibilities. I don't know what that means, but I like the feel of it anyway."

"You're right," Tess said, copying Colette's palms-up position, "it does feel nice."

"Now you both look stupid," I said. I saw my teacher coming out of the classroom at the far end of the hall, walking purposefully toward us. She looked mad. Tess and Colette both turned around and saw her, too.

"Would you rather look stupid or go to the principal?" Colette asked hurriedly.

"I'd rather be a pig," I said. But then I unballed my fists. I didn't hold my arms up like Colette, but I flipped my hands over at my sides.

"I heard a ruckus out here," my teacher said, frowning at me. "Aren't you supposed to be at recess?"

"We're on our way," Tess said, smiling innocently.

"We were just checking to see who got roles in the play," Colette said.

My teacher looked at me skeptically. "Is everything all right?"

"Everything's fine," Colette answered for me; Tess nodded in agreement. And actually, it was. I didn't feel like kicking the wall anymore: the mad had passed.

When I tuned back in to the ICU, the tube was still in Colette's mouth and the needle was still in her arm. Her eyes were still closed, and the machine was still beeping. But I had my palms up, and I felt calmer.

"Frankie?" Mom asked. "Did you hear me?"

"Huh?" I looked at her; she, Tess, and Colette's mom were all looking at me.

"I said we're going to try this again another day," Mom said. "Tess is upset, and you clearly are, too."

"No, I'm okay," I said, glancing back at Colette. She may have done something really mean to me recently, but she'd done other nice things for me in my life. And she'd been playing dare-or-scare again. And right then, remembering the good things, I thought that maybe Tess was right: I thought Colette had been trying to apologize to me. "I want to try to talk to her."

"You do?" Colette's mom asked. She had tears coming down her freckled cheeks, but she looked happy. "Oh, Frankie, thank you so much."

"If you're staying, then I will, too," Tess said.

"I want to do it alone," I said. Tess frowned, so I added, "Then you can have a turn and I'll wait outside."

"Okay." She didn't look like she felt okay. I don't know if she understood that me wanting to talk to Colette alone didn't mean I didn't want her support. I still did, I just didn't want it right next to me.

A nurse came in to check Colette's beeping monitors and then everyone started to leave. Tess was still sniffling, and I felt bad for her. I also felt bad in general because I wasn't the type of person who cried immediately when they saw a hurt friend. I wished I were more like Tess.

"We'll be sitting in those chairs we passed, right by the elevator, okay, Frankie?" Mom said.

"Okay," I said, still standing in the exact spot I'd been in the whole time, at the foot of Colette's bed.

"Are you sure you're okay?"

I thought of what Colette had told the teacher in the hall that day in third grade. "Everything's fine."

chapter 23

Fact: Swelling in the brain is one of
the things that can cause a coma.

"I THINK YOU'VE been really different since Mia moved here," I admitted to Colette. "And you were kind of a jerk that day when you were studying in Tess's room. Not kind of. You were a huge jerk. I've been really mad at you since then."

I knew I probably wouldn't have had the guts to say all that stuff if she'd been awake. I shifted in the chair next to her bed, trying not to look at her face with the tube taped to her cheek.

"It's hard to stay mad at someone when they're hurt, so I'm probably not mad at you anymore, though."

I thought about Colette telling everyone I take tests in a special room—when I don't even do that all the time. I thought about her laughing when Mia had called me a *tornado brain*—making fun of me. I thought about how I'd never say something mean about her behind her back, or to her face.

But then, with a sinking feeling in my belly, I remembered that I had.

Colette's parents were always planning day trips to Portland and Seattle and Olympia, dragging her to indie bookstores and tourist traps. Colette hated it because she was never allowed to bring any friends along. At the end of this past January, just a few weeks before she and Mia had teased me during their study group, Colette had gone on one of the day trips with her parents. The Monday afterward, Colette was standing at my locker when I got to school, excited-emoji face, a wrapped box in her hands.

"I got you a present this weekend!" she said, holding the box out in my direction. She had on a bright green sweater that reminded me of spring even though it was the middle of winter. "I found it in a dusty old bookstore. I had to buy it for you: it's perfect! Open it!"

"Okay . . . ," I said, scrunching my eyebrows together, caught off guard by seeing Colette before school when I normally didn't, by the wrong-season color of her sweater, by her giving me a present on a Monday morning. It was all unexpected. And the honest truth is that I was embarrassed to be receiving a gift in the hallway at school: it was making people look at us—at *me*—and I didn't want to be looked at that day. "It's not my birthday."

"I know when your birthday is, silly." Colette shrugged and shoved the box closer toward me. "I got it for you just because. Open it. I promise you'll like it."

I hate being called *silly*. It always translates into *stupid* in my head.

Mad, I said, "I'll open it later." I turned toward my locker, wanting to shove the box inside so people would stop looking at it as they walked by. I did the combination, but it didn't work on the first try, probably because Colette was distracting me.

"Come on, Frankie, open it now," she said, bouncing up and down. "And tell me about your weekend! Did you go to the—"

"I didn't ask you to get me anything," I interrupted, finally managing to open the locker and throwing the box inside. "And you didn't have to bring it to *school*."

My face was hot. Colette hadn't known, but it'd been a bad morning. The medication I'd been taking was making me feel like my head was going to float off into the sky. I hadn't felt like myself at all.

"Here, I'll just tell you what it is," Colette said. "It's this old board game called Tornado Rex. You're going to love it! You play as a hiker trying to get up a hill before a tornado knocks you—"

"Stop talking about it!" I snapped at her. The hallway was crowded and noisy, so not everyone heard me, but some nearby people did. Colette *definitely* did: she looked like I'd hit her. I should have stopped talking, but it wasn't a day when I could control it. "You're always telling me when to do things," I said. "You think you control my schedule! Stop being so bossy!"

The bell rang; we were late for class. Colette's smile had melted.

She looked at me without saying anything for a few seconds, then shook her head. "That's okay, Frankie, you can open it later."

When I was feeling better after school—after the medication had worn off enough to make me feel like my head was reattached—I'd opened the game and tried it out. And Colette had been right: it *was* perfect. I loved it. I'd texted her: thank you and sorry in one. She'd said it was okay.

But a few weeks later she'd laughed when Mia had called me a name, so maybe it wasn't.

"I guess we both made mistakes," I said to Colette, glancing up at her face, then away again. "I'm sorry." I said the hard word to my shoes. "And I'm sorry I was mean when you came to my room the other night."

It hit me that Colette had probably just waited until I'd gone to do homework at my mom's to come in and take Fred: I never lock my door. And then the whole thing made sense. I imagined it all happening like I was there with her.

Colette fought with her parents about moving.

She came to my room, wanting Fred. When I wouldn't give him to her, she waited and took him anyway. Then she left and did the dune dare, but it was too cold, so she came back and asked Tess for a scarf. She knew she'd need it later.

Then she went to Marsh's, but she ditched her dolphin sweatshirt and scarf for that video because it's always so crazy hot in there. Knowing her next dare was outside, with it getting darker and windier, she borrowed Kai's jacket to layer over her other clothes . . . without asking.

She went to the Sea Witch's house. She went to the school. And then she went . . .

"That was a really stupid thing to do," I said to my friend, filled with regret.

I wished I'd put it all together sooner. I wished I could have helped Colette in time. I tried to think of good memories, when we were younger and the dares and scares were just funny and didn't put anyone in the hospital.

"Hey, remember that time that Tess tried to do that dare where we had to jump over the hurdle at the high school, but she just ran right into it?" I asked. "All three of us couldn't stop laughing," I said to Colette. "Remember?"

I pulled my legs up into the chair and crossed them like a pretzel.

"And remember that time when you rode Tess's favorite horse, Prince, and got so mad because he rolled over to scratch on the sand? And your mom was really mad at you for abandoning the ride when she'd already paid for it?"

I drew a tornado swirl with my fingernail on my knee. "And guess what? You know how you did the ding-dong-ditch dare at the Sea Witch's doorstep—and the kindness dare at the same time, which, by the way, was awesome—well, me and Tess went there, and the Sea Witch totally scared us!"

I laughed because it was more funny than scary now.

"And what about that time when . . ."

I went on and on because talking about dare-or-scare with Colette felt good. Talking with Colette about anything felt good, honestly. Even if I was really just talking *to* Colette.

Sometimes I glanced up at her face, only long enough to make sure she wasn't staring at me. She never was—she didn't open her eyes or move a muscle the whole time I was there. But I had a feeling that she could hear me anyway. I had a feeling that even though we'd both messed up, Colette and I were okay—that we were friends again. And I felt like maybe, in her deep, dark coma dreams, she was laughing with me.

———

AS I WALKED down the hall to tell Tess it was her turn, a flood of memories came back to me—tons of dares Colette,

Tess, and I had done together. *Eat a plate of spaghetti without a utensil. Strut down the hall at school like a model. Walk into a room of people and yell, "Merry Christmas!" when it's the middle of summer.*

I was in my own world—*our* world—and so distracted I was almost run over by two nurses rushing in the opposite direction.

I didn't wonder where they were going then.

I know now.

chapter 24

Myth: You should take shelter
under a bridge during a tornado.

"SEE YOU NEXT time," Gabe said, smiling, holding his acoustic guitar. He'd played it during our session, which I didn't hate. Another thing I didn't hate? Having sessions with Gabe again. Even when they were weird Sunday sessions like today because my mom was worried about me since they'd buried my best friend the day before.

Outside, my mom waited in her car. She was making me go with her to the outlet mall in Seaside to get summer clothes. I think she just wanted to keep an eye on me, like I was going to freak out or something. Tess was in the back seat with earphones on and a sketchbook on her lap, staring out the window of the car with puffy red eyes.

"How did it go?" Mom asked when I was buckled in,

pulling out of the parking space. Someone was waiting to pull in.

"Fine," I said. I opened one of the granola bars Mom keeps in the glove box for me and took a huge bite. "Where's Charles? I thought he was coming with us."

"Tyler called in sick, so Charles had to work the front desk," Mom said, sounding irritated. "What did you and Gabe talk about?"

"Isn't that supposed to be private?" I asked back, my mouth full. I accidentally bit the inside of my cheek.

"Sorry," Mom said. "I just meant . . ."

She didn't finish her sentence, and I didn't ask her to. That wasn't what I wanted to talk about.

"When are the police going to give us back Lemonade?" I asked instead, touching the bite mark on the inside of my cheek with my tongue.

"The bike?" Mom glanced at me with a surprised look, then turned back to the road. "I don't think they will," she said. "I mean, I think it'll go to the dump. It's . . . broken."

"I want it back." I took another bite of granola bar, carefully chewing on the unbitten side, then looked over my shoulder at Tess, who was still staring out the window instead of drawing or talking to us. "I want it back and I want Charles to fix it. I want it to be my bike, not the inn's."

Mom turned the car left at the gas station, toward Highway 101; the outlet mall was a whole state away, in

Oregon. It'd take us fifty minutes to get there but I was looking forward to driving over the Astoria Bridge, which is really, really long and very cool. It's a flat, floating bridge for part and then it climbs high into the sky so ships can go under it. I was thinking about the bridge when Mom finally answered me.

"Frankie, I don't think it's a good idea for you to be riding around on the bike that . . ."

Sort of killed my friend? I thought, but didn't say, because Gabe was helping me remember to keep my filter on, and that would probably be upsetting to Tess and Mom even though it was the truth.

"It *is* a good idea," I said firmly.

"Why?"

"Because it's a connection to Colette," I said. I looked over at my mom; she had tears in her eyes.

"I guess I can understand that," she said, wiping them away. "You're a wonderful girl, do you know that?"

I wasn't sure why she'd said that, and it made me feel weird, so I ignored it. "So can I have the bike?"

"I can't guarantee anything, but I'll ask the police," Mom said. "Should we turn on some music?"

I found a station I liked and reclined my seat a little, watching the landscape go by. There was a long stretch of thick forest like what Colette had ridden through, as we wound our way toward the bottom of Washington. Then the forest opened up and there was the ocean, blue and beautiful and stretching on forever.

As we crossed the bridge, looking out at the sun reflecting off the teal water, I thought of a conversation I'd had earlier with Gabe. I'd told him that everyone had cried at Colette's funeral yesterday, including the preacher, who was probably pretty used to funerals. The kids from school cried. Tess cried the hardest—just like she'd done every day since Colette had died. But I hadn't cried at all. And it had bothered me, until Gabe said something kind of simple: *Everyone grieves differently.*

In most things in life, I'm the outsider. I'm the different one. Or at least it feels that way. But Gabe had said, "Death is the deal breaker. There is no normal when it comes to grief."

There is no normal. Which means there is no abnormal either.

Today, I grieved by being thankful for cool bridges and that I only had a month left of school, instead of thinking about Colette, because today, thinking about her felt shocking and raw and awful.

Other times I thought of her, though, with her huge smile and sometimes-too-loud laugh; of her model poses in pictures; of the way she'd hurt me; of the way I'd hurt her; of the way she'd accidentally died. And I talked to her. Sometimes I grieved by reading Fred and purposely remembering all the times that Colette and I had shared. All the dares. All the birthdays. All the embarrassing moments. All the *everything*.

My grieving wasn't the same every day. And it wasn't the same as anyone else's way of handling it. It wasn't wrong or right. It wasn't abnormal or normal.

It just was.

chapter 25

Fact: It can take years to
recover from a tornado.

THE FIRST WEEK in June, the night before the last day of
seventh grade, I climbed into bed with my phone, then
checked the TwisterLvr feed for recent tornado activity.
It'd been what I'd done every night before bed for forever,
up until Colette had gone missing. I wanted to get my routine back.

"There was an EF2 near Colorado Springs, Colorado," I
said out loud. "It was only on the ground for a few minutes,
though."

"Huh," Tess said from her bedroom. Our doors were
open, so I heard her pencil clink against the others in the
box when she set it down.

"What are you drawing?" I asked.

"Colette," she answered quietly.

"Are you okay?" I asked. The question felt strange on my lips. I was practicing being empathetic.

"I guess?" she said. I didn't know what I was supposed to say next. I listened to the waves crash for a few seconds, thinking about it. But then Tess said, "I'm sad." I heard the scratch of pencil on paper. I don't know why, but I imagined that she was working on getting Colette's eyes right. "Mom thinks I should go to art camp this summer. It's in Boston and I could stay with Aunt Maureen. Mom says it'd be good for me to get away."

"Do you want to go?" I asked, feeling unsettled about the idea of Tess leaving. She was the only friend I had left. I'd be completely alone. Well, except I'd have Kai.

"I don't know," Tess said. "I don't know anything."

"You know more than I do."

"I don't know if I'll ever feel okay again," she said sadly. "I hope so."

"Me too," I said. "I mean, I hope you feel okay again soon. I hope I do, too."

"You will, Frankie," Tess said.

"We can't know for sure," I said because it was the truth, but Tess got quiet. I wondered if that was the wrong response.

Sometimes I wished that Gabe would just give me a script for life or put a bug in my ear and talk me through everything.

Tess and I both went back to what we were doing. Her

pencil scratched on the page and I scrolled more and read about a tornado in a place called Campinas. I opened my internet app to figure out where that was; the app was still on Viewer from when we'd been looking at the dare-or-scare videos. I tapped the address bar, ready to switch to my search engine, when something caught my attention.

A new video had been added to our Viewer account.

"Tess!" I shouted. "Get in here!"

"What's wrong?" she asked from her bed, clearly not moving.

"I'm serious, come here!"

She sighed loudly, and I heard the art book thunk onto the bed. She clomped in from the other room and stopped next to me. She was wearing her pajamas and her hair was unusually messed up.

"Look!" I said, flipping my phone around so she could see. At first I could tell she didn't notice, because when she did, her wide eyes told me so.

"How did that . . . ," she whispered, grabbing my phone so she could scroll through herself.

I thought about it for a minute.

"She's dead," I said.

"God, Frankie, I know," Tess said, shaking her head at me. "Why do you have to—"

"No, I just mean . . . I'm just thinking," I said. "I just mean that she couldn't have uploaded it."

"Fine."

"Should we watch it?"

I took the phone back. "Of course, but, just a second," I said, thinking furiously. "No one else had the password so . . . she would have had to have started uploading it and then—"

"If she started the upload somewhere there wasn't Wi-Fi," Tess said, "then it would have finished when she got a connection again."

"Like if she started at the lighthouse," I said quietly.

"And didn't make it back to civilization."

We both stared at my phone.

"The upload date is two years ago," I said, pointing at the screen. "She must have changed it again."

"I wish we knew why she kept doing that," Tess said.

"I told you. She did it so we wouldn't see an alert. She probably wanted to surprise us with the videos."

"You never told me that," Tess said. She didn't sound mad, just matter-of-fact. "You told me something about Kai and Dillon and their skateboarding channel."

"Yeah, but . . ." I thought back, trying to remember. I know I'd connected the dots from Kai about why she'd change the dates, understanding that it meant Colette had wanted to keep the videos secret from us. And I thought I'd said that to Tess. But now I couldn't remember doing it.

"Did I tell you that Viewer automatically archives videos

after three years?" I asked. "So our old ones aren't gone forever . . . they're just in the cloud or whatever."

"*I* told *you* that," Tess said, shaking her head.

Tess sat down on my bed next to me, which bothered me, but I didn't make her get off. I figured she wouldn't be there too long. I told myself not to say anything.

Tess leaned closer so she could see the video. I double tapped to start it, neither of us saying anything about how she was alive in this video, and not alive now.

"Turn on your sound," Tess whispered. "She's talking."

"It is on, there's no sound on the videos," I whispered back.

Tess tsked and took the phone from me, messed with it, then handed it back. She rewound the video and hit play, and the sound of Colette's voice startled me.

"How did you do that?" I asked.

"Shhh!" Tess said, and I didn't get mad, because I wanted to hear what Colette was saying in the video, too.

"I want you to know that this dare is terrifying!" Colette said with a laugh. She was on the bike path, holding the camera out from her face. She wasn't wearing a helmet. "Here goes nothing!"

She turned the video on fast motion through her ride. Tess and I were squished together, her biting her nails loudly, me too sucked in by the video to care about Tess's touch or nails or her being on my bed in the first place. I was scared that we'd see Colette go off the road, but instead, in an instant, the fast motion stopped, and Colette was at the lighthouse. She'd made it.

I was letting that thought wash over me when I heard her say, "Frankie, I don't know how you did this like it was nothing—and as a younger kid! You're really brave, my friend." She looked around again. "Okay, that's it for this one."

The video clicked off.

I felt Tess crying next to me, her shoulders shaking and the force of it vibrating my whole bed.

"I'm sorry," I said. "I shouldn't have told you I found it."

"No, it's okay," she said through her tears. "It's good to see her again." Then she asked, wiping her eyes and sniffing, "That's it? There aren't any more?"

"I guess not," I said, scrolling down the page to make sure. "No, that's all."

I scooted over a little to give us both some room. Tess hugged one of my pillows. I didn't want her to, but I didn't say anything because I knew she probably needed the comfort. She wiped her cheeks again with her arm. She was going to get my pillow wet, I knew it. She stared into space, sniffing. I hadn't turned on the lamp, so the room had gotten dark and it made me tired. I scooted close to the wall and leaned back on my other pillow.

"Can I sleep in your room tonight?" she asked. I didn't

answer right away, so Tess said, "It's okay, Frankie, I know you don't like people in your room."

No, I don't.

But you're different.

But you kick!

Also, my space is my space.

But you're so sad.

And I'm sad, too.

The sides of my brain fought for so long that Tess started to get up.

"Wait," I said, not wanting to be mean or insensitive. Wanting to be there for her when she needed me. Wanting to be a friend to my sister.

"It's okay," Tess said again. She looked miserable. "I'll see you in the morning."

I wanted to be someone who could say yes immediately. Who didn't think about how weird it would be to sleep next to another person, even my sister. Other girls had sleepovers—I never did. I wanted to be the girl who had sleepovers.

"Wait, Tess," I said, standing up, thinking of a compromise where someone else wouldn't be in my space— touching my stuff. "Let's sleep in your room."

epilogue

BEFORE SCHOOL ON the first day of eighth grade, I was out on the beach, sitting on a washed-up log while Pirate chased pipers near the water.

I took out my phone and opened Viewer. I purposely hadn't checked it all summer because seeing Colette alive when she wasn't anymore had felt too painful, but I'd promised myself I'd look again before school started, to remember her. School would start in minutes, so I was out of time: I had to look.

I cranked the phone's volume up all the way, feeling stupid that I'd thought there wasn't sound on any of the videos—and thankful that Tess had fixed my phone. With the sound on, I watched the video of the last dare Colette ever did—the ride to the lighthouse—feeling happy when she called me brave. I watched the other videos, too, like her running through the beach grass with the thud of the hollow ground as she ran by, me imagining her jumping off the dune and wondering how far she got before she landed. And then I opened the video where she was singing at school, fast-forwarding past the talking part to the song.

She stood at center court in the gym, singing full volume into a portable microphone she'd had forever. I'd heard her sing before and wasn't shocked by her nice voice.

What she sang, though, that was another story.

Last year, about this time, a bunch of kids from school had set up a bonfire on the beach to celebrate the end of summer. Colette and Tess had forced me to go: I'd wanted to stay in and watch *Tornado Ally*. But they'd bribed me with marshmallows.

Someone had brought a portable speaker and was streaming music. A dad of one of the kids was lurking off to the side in a shelter, looking at his phone. He'd started the fire and had been designated chaperone, I guess.

When Tess, Colette, and I had arrived, we searched for sticks, then put down our blanket and started toasting marshmallows. There were probably twelve or thirteen kids there including us, Mia, Colin, Bryce, and Marcus from homeroom, who was always getting in trouble. That night, we'd all watched as he'd picked up a live crab and chased Mia with it, then gotten scolded by the lurking parent.

Anyway, Kai had been there, too. I'd noticed him through the fire, right when the playlist changed to a song that now I'll probably never forget in my life. You know those songs that feel like they're controlling your emotions? It was one of those.

"You like him, don't you?" Colette had asked, too quietly for anyone else to hear. I'd kept my eyes on Kai, watching him laughing with Dillon about dropping a marshmallow in the sand, daring him to eat it. "Frankie, you do, right?"

I hadn't said anything at first. But something about the song and the warm summer night and the ocean next to me and the stars overhead had made me someone else for a second—someone who could easily identify her emotions.

"Maybe," I'd whispered to Colette. She was the only person I'd ever come close to admitting that to, and that *maybe* had been a big deal to me.

I guess Colette had known it was a big deal, too.

I rewound to the beginning to hear Colette talk.

"Frankie, I have something to say, okay?" She backed away from where she'd propped the phone, stumbling a little on the freshly polished gym floor.

"I'm going to do the dare in a second, but first, I know you're mad at me." Colette looked down at her scuffed white sneakers—I'd been right about those, too. "I'm pretty sure I know why, and I feel really bad about it." She looked up again, her face concerned. "I hope that when you watch these videos of our old dares, you'll see that I'm sorry. It was the best thing I could think to do for you, so you'd know how much I miss our friendship. This weird game you made up was one of my favorite things we ever did together. And I hope seeing it again will make you want to be friends again, because I'm moving soon, and I won't be able to stand it if you're still mad at me."

She looked at the floor and sniffed, then took a deep breath. She tugged down the hem of her T-shirt, tossed her bright red hair over her shoulder, and cleared her throat. She looked around, probably to make sure she was alone.

"Okay, Frankie, this song is for you."

And then she sang my song for Kai.

Even though it was Colette singing and not the real band, it made me feel squishy in the same way that I had last year. And watching Colette sing like she was on a reality show after sneaking into our school, watching her go full-out, I felt braver about school starting. I felt braver about everything. I felt inspired by her.

I wiped away the salty tears that had finally come in their own time, just like Gabe had said they would. I threw the stick Pirate had just dropped at my feet, then I texted Kai.

FRANKIE

His reply came back quickly.

KAI

Sup!

How was ur summer?

Mostly good

Are you excited for school???

I'm excited to not be at the retirement village anymore

So many old people

I mean they're cool but

My Gpops made me play cards every single day

LOL

So, I was wondering . . .

???

Um . . . ur typing a long time

K now I'm nervous

Frankie?

I might have to call you Frances to get your attention . . .

Back!

Pirate wanted me to throw her stick

NEVER CALL ME FRANCES

LOL, got it

So . . . what's the ???

I took a deep breath.

I was just going to ask . . .

Wanna do a dare with me sometime?

It took almost no time at all for him to reply.

YES.

Today

?

My belly and cheeks both felt warm, and I was glad that I was the only person on the beach and that dogs don't care if you're embarrassed.

Meet later at the frying pan after school . . . 4?

K!!

I sent him a thumbs-up emoji, then he sent a smile emoji back, then even though I wanted to send him fifty more, I put my phone away, thinking Gabe would be proud of me for stopping the conversation.

I didn't know this then since I'm not psychic, but later, Kai would ask me to hold his hand—and I would for a whole minute without freaking out about touching another person, because Kai isn't just any other person. He's Kai. And holding his hand would feel awkward but nice, and less disgusting than I would have imagined.

The reason I could do that is because of change. Change used to be my enemy because I'd thought it was always bad. For sure, there'd been a lot of bad change that'd happened lately. But there'd been a little bit of good change, too: change in me. Sitting on the log, smiling about Kai like my cheeks were going to break, I felt mostly ready to start eighth grade. I felt older. I felt less alone. I felt okay.

And I felt okay that I didn't feel okay about Colette.

I used to try to just deal with things and move on. It's not worth it to think about sad things, like getting teased by kids you don't know. (It's harder when you're being made fun of by kids you do know.) But I used to try to just handle a situation and then forget it if I could. I'm sure Gabe would tell me an official therapy word for that if I asked him.

But Colette . . . Her death was a sad thing I couldn't move on from easily. I didn't know how long losing her would feel like a boulder on my chest—maybe forever. But the thing that made it the tiniest bit better was that now I knew that I hadn't ever really lost her friendship. That made it okay for me to feel not okay—for as long as I needed to.

"I miss you," I said to Colette, hoping the ocean wind would carry my message off to her, wherever she was. I waited a little bit, to see if a message came back. None did, but I still felt like maybe she'd heard me.

I stood up and stretched, ready to go back to the inn to get my backpack for school. Before I called for Pirate, before I started whatever was coming next, I waited just a few seconds longer still. Something felt different about my body: something felt better.

I looked down at my hands and realized that, without knowing it, I'd flipped them over, so the backs of my hands were against my jeans.

Facing the ocean, on the beach where we'd spent so much of our time together, feeling both okay and not okay, I stood as my friend Colette had told me to.

I stood with my palms up.

Author's Note

NEURODIVERGENT IS A newish term for people living with developmental disabilities such as dyslexia, attention deficit hyperactivity disorder (ADHD), Tourette's syndrome, and obsessive-compulsive disorder, and for those on the autism spectrum. I hadn't heard of or used the word until I wrote *Tornado Brain,* despite knowing and loving several people who fall into this category. Instead, I describe them using positive terms like bright, creative, hilarious, curious, and inventive.

That's not always how they describe themselves, though, because living with a developmental disability can make people feel the opposite of bright, inventive, or curious. They can feel stupid, different, weird in a bad way, and disconnected. According to the Centers for Disease Control and Prevention, about one in six of the 74.2 million children in the United States have a developmental disability, so they're not alone—but it doesn't mean they don't feel that way.

My wish is that *Tornado Brain* helps neurodivergent readers feel more connected. Frankie sees the world in a unique way—I hope readers gain a new perspective from her story. And I hope *Tornado Brain* reminds neurotypical readers to practice empathy. Neurodivergence is invisible; reading more books featuring neurodivergent characters is a step toward understanding.

A *Wired* magazine article from 2013 said, "In a world changing faster than ever, honoring and nurturing neurodiversity is civilization's best chance to thrive in an uncertain future."

Civilization's best chance to thrive.

There's nothing stupid about that.

Acknowledgments

IF YOU'RE A person who reads acknowledgments, you're my kind of person. Even still, I'll attempt to keep this brief.

Thank you to the team that helped make *Tornado Brain* happen, including Dan Lazar, Cecilia De La Campa, Torie Doherty-Munro, and Alessandra Birch at Writers House; and Stacey Barney, Jen Klonsky, Chandra Wohleber, Caitlin Tutterow, Vanessa DeJesús, and the entire marketing, sales, and publicity machine at G. P. Putnam's Sons. Stacey and Jen, our conference call the day the book landed at Putnam is tucked into my heart for keeps. Thank you, also, to the thoughtful agents and editors around the globe who've connected with Frankie and introduced her to readers far away.

Special thanks to the contributors of several websites for reminding me of tornado facts I learned as a kid or teaching me new ones, including *National Geographic*, *HowStuffWorks*, *Scientific American*, *LiveScience*, and *Weather.com*. To *Superbetter* author Jane McGonigal for introducing me to the idea of turning my palms up to feel less stressed. And to my sister for leaving *Superbetter* on my doorstep precisely when I needed it.

Speaking of sisters, I'd also like to thank my village . . . my siblings and siblings-in-law, parents, aunts and uncles, nieces and nephews, co-parent extraordinaire, century-old grandpa, and the rest of the branches of my family tree— blood or not—in Oregon, California, Wyoming, Colorado, and, of course, Washington.

On the topic of The Evergreen State, I must thank the residents of the town of Long Beach for cultivating such a perfect setting for Frankie's world. Like something a middle schooler might write in a friend's yearbook, "Never change."

You either, Jon. For me, Long Beach equals you. Thank you for introducing me to my happy place and for making it even better, lighting fires in the rain, patiently detangling kites, leading bike tours, committing to reconnaissance missions, and laughing with me when Clue is the most terrifying game on Earth. Thank you for being there through the emotional birth of this book, and always.

And especially, thank you to my daughters. You are, simply, my everything. You inspire me and support me in a way no one else can—L, with your creativity and honesty, and C, with your constant encouragement and editor's eye. This is our book, and it wouldn't have happened without you. I love you both more than you can imagine.

Finally, I want to thank the Frankies out there for striving to thrive in a world that wasn't built with you in mind. Life can be challenging when you think differently. Though it may feel like it sometimes, you are not alone.

Together we can embrace our differences. We can celebrate the creative genius and unique perspectives of people like Frankie instead of trying to shove everyone into the same box. Because if you ask me, if we were all the same, we'd make up a dreadfully boring box.

So thank you, reader, for being uniquely you.

Whatever brand of brain you've got.